UNNATURAL SECRETS

BONNIE ELIZABETH

My Big Fat Orange Cat Publishing

Unnatural Secrets
My Big Fat Orange Cat
Gothic/Occult Horror September 2018

Copyright 2018
Bonnie Elizabeth Koenig

Cover image Copyright © "FairyTale Design" | Deposit Photo
Cover Copyright © Bonnie Elizabeth Koenig

My Big Fat Orange Cat Publishing
MyBigFatOrangeCat.com

ISBN : 978-1-953363-08-4 trade paperback

I had the dream again. I was running through the depths of Kernroote Castle, into places that should have been underground, places that should have existed only in horror movies, but yet I was there, barefoot and running, a filmy nightgown of the sort I'd never choose flying around my body, making me easy prey for hands to reach out and grab.

Except, of course, there were no hands reaching for me. I knew that. I tripped over a large root in the floor but I got up and kept running, oddly disturbed by my fall. The ground was dirt, after all, but what sort of large tree would send roots so deep into the earth that they infiltrated a cellar?

My mind tried to wrap itself around the question even as I ran. I had a sense that this was a dream, but there was a realness to it that said it had happened before, or would happen soon. I kept running.

There was no sound in the chambers I ran through. No smell. My breath came easier than I would have expected.

I was cold, despite the exercise. I had no idea what was chasing me and I couldn't look back, not again.

I tripped over another root, landing in front of the first door I had seen, light brown wood that looked old and ready to rot away. Metal bands fitted the top and bottom, tarnished but still in solid condition. A fog leaked from behind the door, reaching out to me.

I scrambled backwards, not able to move fast enough. In my dream I screamed, bringing the thing that had chased me to the door.

I looked up, seeing a man with the dark eyes. I knew him. Shock washed through me. It couldn't be him.

I closed my eyes against the knowledge, the certainty of what was going on, that my life was in more mortal peril than I had thought, and when I opened them again I was in my bedroom, more than a thousand miles away, tucked in an apartment complex that was never silent.

I settled my breathing, thankful for the sounds of cars passing along the road outside, though it was late. My upstairs neighbor thumped across the floor of his apartment. I had no idea why he appeared to have to hop across the floor rather than walk like normal people.

One of my neighbors was smoking and I caught the sweet smell of pot floating around the bedroom; just a trace, but enough to tell me that I wasn't alone. I should go purchase some. Maybe I'd sleep better. I'd had that thought before but never gotten around to it. The idea of not being in control was almost as frightening as the nightmare.

Because when I was awake, I knew that so much of the nightmare was true. A memory.

Chapter 2

If you live in North Carolina long enough, you hear about the Biltmore Estate, probably even visit it, perhaps own annual passes to enjoy the gardens for a long walk whenever you wish. But you can go your whole life and never hear of Kernroote Castle, which is perhaps an hour north and west of the famed estate.

The Kernroote family, of course, have never been philanthropists, nor, as far as I've been able to tell, have they ever needed money, not really. But in the last decade, someone decided to open the place up as a sort of boutique hotel. "Bed-and-breakfast" wouldn't do it justice. The place was too large and ornate, although they do offer a fine breakfast in addition to a quite comfortable bed.

I hadn't heard of it until my sister, Kara, suggested the castle as a place I could go to write my novel and hide from the world after Daniel, my loving husband of ten years, decided in our eleventh year to become less than loving and run off with his secretary. A trite story, made even more trite by the fact that she was indeed ten years his junior. Buying me off, he left me with a tidy alimony, although I've heard such things are not done so much these days. However, it gave me some time to hide and recover and decide who I was now that I was nearing forty with no husband and wasn't likely to have the children I once longed for.

I had dreamed of being a writer all my life. I'd submitted stories here and there to magazines and started collecting a tidy pile of rejection slips. I'd also hoped to get pregnant but picked up a parental rejection slip each and every month like clockwork. Each time I learned of another failure I began to fall into a tailspin, one that even Daniel's kindness couldn't work me out of.

He used my pain as an excuse for his affair.

Then he used my pain as an excuse for leaving me.

If I had believed his excuses at all, I stopped when I learned that his soon-to-be new wife was already six months along when we divorced. Children were apparently in *his* future, along with a new Mrs. Holland, leaving me back as Becca Winter. I couldn't bear keeping his name.

So writing it would be. The book would be my baby. There was really nothing to hold me in the city. North Carolina, Charlotte in particular, was Daniel's home. Not mine.

I was an army brat who called no place home, exactly. I loved the mountain air and the cool weather. I had skied before we met and perhaps I'd move off to Colorado to start a new life, but first I would finish my book.

"Kernroote Castle is a little-known boutique hotel nestled in the mountains to the west of Asheville, North Carolina," my sister read from the website over the phone.

"What are we talking about?" I asked.

"The perfect place for you to run away to write your book. Daniel's alimony is enough that you can take your portion of the condo sale and use it to stay at Kernroote for three months or so while you write," Kara said reasonably. "It's not like you'll have to worry. Quit your job. You hate it. Maybe you'll make friends there and find something you do enjoy even if you don't end up writing the book."

Kara always had a fallback plan, so I didn't take it as a sign of little faith that she didn't think I could write a book. If she were to take such a leap, she'd want a dozen plans in place for *just in case*. Her penchant hadn't helped her in the romance department, as she'd been proposed to six times all by different men and each time she'd fled to a new city. She's a nurse so she had no problem finding jobs.

I, however, a practical business major, had struggled because everyone was a business major and until you got some good experience, finding a job was hard. Even then, trying to keep a salary of any sort was tough, especially if you didn't have a solid career goal. Something I could do at Kernroote Castle was research the types of industry I was likely to find in Colorado and educate myself on the main companies. I had some of the money stashed so even if I had to wait a few years, I could make. Eventually, I'd find something.

I'd seen the pictures of Kernroote Castle online but they didn't do the place justice any more than the pictures of the Biltmore did justice to it, which I realized a month later as I drove my car through the tall metal gates with the large K centered in them. They were black and shone as if someone had just repainted them. As the castle had opened to the public only a year ago, it had probably been barely that long since the painting.

Once through the heavy wrought iron gates, which were attached to a stone wall that was at least the five feet high, perhaps higher, I drove on a long, fairly narrow graveled drive. It meandered through trees and down a slope and then around the side of a low hill. I couldn't hear the cars on the main road I'd turned off any longer. Just five minutes ago I'd been on the outskirts of Asheville, floating through the beginning of rush hour traffic, and now here I was, practically alone.

No other cars passed me, which was good, as I worried that if another car did come along, there wasn't room to pass. Perhaps there was another way out of the place. Certainly if they had guests there with any regularity, they should widen the drive, or perhaps it was a road. It was long enough that I wasn't sure what to call it. But it was an accident waiting to happen, particularly the way drivers seemed to drive in the southern part of North Carolina.

The trees got closer together, as if the entry was a clearing and now I was seeing the real landscape. It darkened as if I had gone from a late August afternoon to evening in the space of quarter of a mile. Though the driving was slow going, it was nowhere near *that* slow.

I was about to turn on my headlights when the trees became sparser and I rounded another bend and drove up a hill. The trees on the hill were spaced in orderly rows with no underbrush. It looked like a small orchard. At the top, the road curved to the right, with more trees—a thicket of some sort—and I rounded around until I came to a place where the road began to slope down.

The trees parted before me and I was presented my first view of the castle. "Castle" was an apt word, though there are few true castles in the United States. This was a castle on the scale of the Banff Springs Hotel. I suspected that even the Springs was dwarfed by this, although having never been there, I supposed it could have been the way the juxtaposition of the Canadian Rocky backdrop compared to the Great Smokey Mountains.

Great though the mountains are, they are not the Canadian Rockies.

I counted four rounded towers, two near the entrance and two at what would be the corners. I drove slowly down the curving road to the parking area.

As I got closer, I noted the sanded, gray stone bricks that made up the place. There were patches in places that looked to be modern cement but in general the place was in fine repair. There was a huge portico in the front, clearly added recently for it was in wood and red brick, not gray. Of course, I did see red brick accents in places. A planter lined the front of the castle, also in red brick, delineating the space between the parking area, which was gravel, and the building itself.

The parking area angled up a degree or two to go under the portico. A man in a white uniform stood outside, looking bored. So not everything was royal at the place.

The dark wood beneath the portico blocked out the last of the sun and it was dark enough under there that I had a hard time finding the case for my sunglasses. I turned off the engine and stepped out. The white-uniformed man had come over to the side of my car by this time.

"Are you checking in?" He asked.

"I am," I said.

"I can get your bags if you'll open the trunk." He gestured to the back of the car.

I reached in and popped the trunk. He walked back to see my two large suitcases. I grabbed my handbag and the computer bag I was carrying in the back. I could come back for the two bags of groceries I'd stashed in the car. While I'd eat out most of the time, it was always good to have snacks.

Though the hotel website had advertised it being just a

short trip from Asheville, I hadn't wanted to count on having a place where I could shop easily. I might not have to worry about money for a while—even with this trip, I was socking away half my alimony each month—but I hated to pay more than I needed to for general purchases.

I followed the uniformed man inside as he pulled both my suitcases over to one of the shiny silver carts so common in hotels. He piled both of them on there.

"Will your husband be meeting you later?" he asked, quite formally.

"I'm not married," I said.

He blanched a little as if having said something wrong and then, without an apology or anything else, he turned his back and pushed the cart through the large doors. The first set of doors were glass, the sort of sliding doors that you find in a typical hotel entry area. The next set, just beyond that entry, were tall wooden doors that reached up two stories, at least. Each dark wood door was carved with the image of a tree, a huge tree with branches that twined and twisted from near the bottom to the top. Even the roots were tangled and twisted. Each reached towards the other door as if the two trees were lovers separated for all eternity.

The uniformed man opened the door, giving it a hard tug. It opened slowly as if on a mechanized opener. To the side, I saw that there was a smaller glass door that would open and close as well. No doubt the wood doors were for show.

As we passed through the doors, I marveled that the wood was probably two inches thick. I wanted to run my hands over it, but I kept them to myself. That was probably good, given the look from the man behind the desk that sat in what had once been an elegant private entry hall.

To my right a stairwell curved up and around the entry,

pausing at a landing to each floor, and I counted five, although the first floor appeared to be two stories high. The wood accents were all dark mahogany brown. The floor was the same dark wood, though there were plenty of black stains and a few places where it looked lighter as if someone had replaced pieces recently. It was all covered with large Persian-style carpets in a pale moss green, cream, and pink.

Large square chairs in cream were scattered around the room, next to creamy white round end tables. On several of the tables sat fresh cut flowers that picked up the colors of the carpets. On the whole, the entry was a pleasant affair, made brighter by whoever had decorated the place. In other colors, the place could have been dark and gloomy.

The man behind the desk, which was done in the same mahogany dark wood with no green and cream to brighten it, darkened the whole place with the attitude he projected onto the entry. Shadows covered his face and he appeared disapproving.

"Ms. Winter?" the man asked, his voice bored and vaguely critical. His eyes were hidden beneath heavy lids but from what I could see of them, they appeared dark as the shadows behind which he hid.

"Yes." I was slightly uncomfortable. I'd never been greeted in such away.

"Very good." He made a nod. "We'll need the information on your car and then we'll need to process your credit card. I see you'll be staying here for quite some time. Would you rather pay all at once or shall I charge your card weekly or monthly?"

I answered as best I could, thinking that perhaps it was my unusually long stay that had made him familiar with my name. Of course, it was early evening and there were only four cars in the lot. Perhaps the place was too new to be filled to capacity. Besides, it was mid-week and people might prefer to come here only on weekends.

Signing my name on the familiar hotel receipts and filling out the license plate number of my car, I had to laugh to think that this was a boutique hotel. If they used half of this place, it wasn't boutique by any means. There were Holiday Inns that were barely a quarter of the size.

"The elevator is around the corner," the man pointed to his right, my left. The hall there was narrower, made so by the large desk. If he hadn't pointed it out, I would have expected that it was an employee-only area. Still, there were narrow windows that ran from the floor to the ceiling so it wasn't as dark as it might have been, though the glass was mullioned with dark metal.

"Thank you," I said, taking the key, which was a modern card that seemed out of place in this castle. There was the folded paper envelope with a pocket for storing the key and an extra, in case I invited someone with me who needed another key, along with directions on how to access the Wi-Fi. I had known, from checking online, that the place had Wi-Fi; still, the simple reminder surprised me, here in this place that seemed from another era.

Giving the man at the desk a smile, I let the uniformed man lead the way down the hall towards the elevator.

It was a short walk. Next to the elevators were two vending machines, one of bottled water and one of soda. The floors remained covered by the green-and-cream rugs. In the third narrow window, a white Grecian-style urn that came up nearly to my waist sat, with fake pink-and-cream flowers with petals like chrysanthemums, though I have to admit to never having seen a mum that large or quite so ornate. There were pale green leaves tucked in the urn as well.

I had but a moment to take in the gold sheen of the elevator doors before they slid open with barely a whisper. The hush suggested that these were new. The interiors were dark paneled to the waist and then mirrored above that. The carpet on the floor was a surprising black, as if the green and cream was too fancy for the elevator. One wouldn't want people to stay in there, would they?

It was a roomy enough cube even with the luggage cart that the uniformed man pulled in. I pressed the button for the fifth floor. I had counted five floors but there were actually seven buttons in the elevator as well as a basement and what must be a subbasement. I could forgive myself for not counting the lower levels, but I was surprised that there were two floors above mine. I'd have to go outside and recount, probably when I went to park my car.

"How long have you worked here?" I asked the man pleasantly.

He looked at me for a moment longer than I would have expected before he responded. "Since they opened about eleven months ago."

"Do you like it?" I pressed.

Again, that slow response. The elevator doors opened onto a short hallway. This hall was carpeted, not just covered in rugs. The carpets here were darker green with cream flecks, brighter than many industrial carpets, but of their ilk.

"It's okay," the uniformed man said, pulling the cart out of the elevator. I looked for a sign and saw that my room, 535, was to the left of the elevator.

I went that way, passing the top of the very long stairs looking down towards the lobby. It seemed further away than just five floors and I had no desire to linger there. I got the faintest whiff of cooking meat and wondered if I'd spend my nights salivating to the smells of steak and crab being cooked at the bar restaurant that sat on the premises.

The short hall turned inward and then another hallway went to the right, still covered in the same carpet. It was so thick and soft that my feet sank into it as if they were sinking into fresh snow. The walls here remained dark, mahogany paneling covering the lower half of the wall and then green-and-cream wallpaper on the upper half.

The lights were bright but that did nothing to illuminate the darker shadows near the base of the walls. The hall was narrower than I expected in such a posh hotel, but then again, this had been built a very long time ago. In fact, though I'd researched it and talked with Kara about it, I hadn't been able to find anything to suggest when it had been built.

Just past every third door there was a painting that looked like the typical mountain scenes in many hotels. There was nothing to differentiate these. It was all clean and clear, as if someone had spent time making this look as typical of a hotel as possible. I wondered if all the floors had hallways as narrow as this. The poor porter couldn't have stepped around the cart if he'd wanted to.

My room was halfway down the hallway on the left side. I'd be looking out the back, then. I opened it, not sure what to expect; the pictures I'd remembered from the website were all a blur between what I had seen and hadn't.

The door opened, as doors in so many hotel rooms did, into a small foyer with the bathroom off to the left and a closet to the right. There was a surprising amount of room in the foyer, given how narrow the hall was. The closet was practically a walk-in closet. I only glanced in the bathroom, where I saw cream tiles and a sink with plenty of counter far deeper into a space than I had expected.

Beyond that, which was a bit further than in the average hotel, I came to a sitting area with a small wet bar that included a microwave and a coffee pot. A sofa and a recliner sat off to the left of the room. The recliner was done in plain cream leather, the sofa done in a floral brocade, but both looked well-stuffed and comfortable. A coffee table rested between them. Beyond that was a low wall and a curtain that could be pulled all the way across the opening. Now, the curtain was open, showing the bedroom area, which held a bed that was at least a king size and another recliner, a small, typical hotel desk, and a flat-screen television.

Then there were the French doors, covered in light sheers, behind which were two room-darkening shades that could be pulled. I was drawn immediately to the doors to look out. There was a large stone balcony, worthy of a fantasy-world king, waiting for me. There were similar balconies all along as I looked out and around.

"This is wonderful," I said to the uniformed man. I pulled out some money from my purse and pressed it on him. He'd already taken my two large suitcases and set them off the cart, which he was wheeling out to the hallway.

He nodded at me, not saying thank you. I closed the door after him. What a strange place.

I listened as the cart squeaked a bit as it rolled down the softly carpeted corridor. I didn't hear a thing from the man in uniform. In fact, it was so silent in the room that I could have been alone in the building. It was almost creepy, particularly when I remembered what the place looked like.

Still, it was an amazing room both in size and the fact that there was a large window to one side of the French doors. When I worked at the desk, I could look out the window and enjoy the view, which is exactly what I determined to do.

I slipped out onto the balcony, taking my phone. There were two outdoor chairs with large cushions tied to them outside. The cushions were still green and cream and pink, pulling the color scheme outside.

Looking out over the back of the castle, I saw that there were two wings to either side. All the fifth-floor rooms in the center had these large balconies. There were balconies on the fourth floor on the wing to my left and I saw no balconies to my right, although on the ground it appeared that someone had created a sort of private garden area for each room on the main floor. In the center, I saw concrete steps leading down to a large garden with a pond in the center. It was almost a maze with gravel paths and assortment of bushes that held the last of summer's blooms. No doubt before I left, someone would come by to trim them.

Around the building I saw the rising of the mountains in the area, all rounded hills. Most of the trees that graced the slopes were still full green, but here and there, a few were already beginning to turn shades of yellow and even orange. There were more than the usual number of firs as well, but those would make the place interesting even in the winter.

A breeze blew through and it was chillier than I liked. I quickly took photos for my sister and to post on my social media accounts to brag about where I was staying. Who knew this place was even here? In addition, the price was clearly right for the size of the room.

I slipped back inside, noticing as I did where the shadows fell in the corners. Like in all hotel rooms, the light wasn't bright enough to banish them all. Still, it seemed a pleasant enough place, if a bit too quiet. There was a clock radio near the bed and I fiddled with that, figuring I'd find my MP3 player when I unpacked.

But first, I wanted to bring up my groceries and move my car.

I made sure I had my purse and my keys, both for the car and the room, and I left. I heard someone upstairs, making me wonder about the sixth and seventh floors. The large stairwell had ended at the fifth floor with no more stairs going up. Perhaps the upper two floors were for family or staff or storage. Even just one wing of the building would comfortably house a large family or even two.

The hallway was empty, as it had been earlier. I walked quickly down it, listening slightly for any sound of music or television from the behind the doors, but I heard nothing. I had to wait for the elevator but it wasn't a long wait. I rode down alone.

On the main floor, I stepped into the narrow hall. Through the long narrow windows I noted the four cars in the parking lot. If that was all of us in the place, then perhaps I was alone on the fifth floor, unless someone stayed on the sixth. I considered asking at the front desk, but the man who had been there wasn't around.

I poked my head into the main entry area. A fireplace was on the wall I hadn't gotten a good look at. It was the sort that you could walk into if you had such a desire and it was open but for a decorative grate in front of it. There was a step built of gray stone and the surrounding area was all stone, decoratively placed. It was a thing of beauty, really, and captured my attention for longer than it should have.

I turned to look out at the back area and saw a large room filled with windows and white rattan furniture. The green-and-cream color scheme filled that area was well. It was clearly where one would sit and eat some breakfast. I wandered in, though the lights were off and it made the entire room shadowy and pink as the early evening sun set across the place. More French doors opened on the far side of the large room, just to the left of the eating area. They led out to a concrete patio that appeared to run the length of the main part of the building with the low wide stairs I had seen from my room going down to the garden. From this lower vantage, I couldn't see the pond at all.

I considered going outside but decided against it. I needed to move my car and there would be time enough to explore the grounds tomorrow and perhaps get inspiration for my book.

I walked back through the entry, noting that the desk clerk was still not at the desk, passed through the small glass door to the side of the large ones, and exited to the front. The uniformed man stood to one side, talking on a Bluetooth headset. He nodded at me but didn't smile.

I nodded back and got into my car. I moved it around the corner into the parking lot, next to the last car in the line. I dug through the back, picking out my two bags of groceries, and brought them inside. The porter had his back to me, listening intently to his conversation, decidedly unfriendly to the guests, or at any rate, me.

At least the birds were chirping and the late summer cicadas were playing their instrumentals while I was out. Nature was clearly more friendly than the staff at Kernroote Castle.

Inside, silence greeted me. It would have been welcoming had they thought to put music on—even the low elevator sort of music that made up background noise would have been welcome. This was like coming home to an empty house and about as inviting. There was still no desk clerk. In fact, I noticed, there wasn't even a bell in case one had a need or a question. I shook my head. I guess that was one reason the rooms, while spendy, were relatively cheap for what you got.

I walked through the entry and towards the elevators. It was as if the place didn't quite exist. I might be in a dream. The shadows that moved in corners were decidedly creepy and felt like the beginnings of a nightmare. The silence made the place that much more surreal. Even the fact that the scent was so neutral it didn't seem to be there made the place feel more dreamlike.

I got in the elevator and rode up. It was too silent. What I wouldn't have given for a creak or a groan or some old Abba song slowed down by half and played on violins. At least on my floor the smells from the restaurant kitchen drifted up, although the surreal feeling of the place made me wonder what kind of meat, exactly, they were cooking.

More emptiness on the fifth floor. I had stayed in hotels before and I knew that you didn't always notice people, but there was a sense when a place is mostly empty, and this place gave off that feeling. I passed through the too-narrow hallway, noting where the shadows fell, planning to see if they fell in the same place in the morning.

I opened my room door. For a moment the room wasn't at all what I expected. It was darker and there was no green-and-gray carpet. I saw mahogany wood floor and walls, rather than the moss-green color the room was painted. The place was tiny and shrouded in shadows. Then I was in my room, the large open foyer followed by the sitting area and finally the bedroom.

I shook my head a little at my fancy. Certainly the darkened room was kind of what I had expected the first time I walked in. Now I knew better. Still, it bothered me that my imagination was already running wild.

I put my groceries away in the refrigerator, which was

compact but seemed cool enough. There were two bottles of water with a sign that said Complimentary. There were definitely some nice little touches.

I moved on to putting my clothing away in the closet. Deep inside the walk-in closet I thought I heard a knock at the door. I finished hanging my blouse and walked out to the door, but there was no one in the hallway. I opened the door anyway, looking to see if someone was walking away, but saw nothing.

No doubt my imagination was working overtime. It was why I thought I might make a writer after all. I was always imagining things, making up stories about people that I saw walking into movie theaters and restaurants. I could spin a tale of a couple looking serious at dinner all evening.

The husband in the jacket was actually a spy. The fact that his jacket was too large yet he wore it at the table meant he carried a gun he didn't want anyone to know about. She was a spy too, his secret lover, and perhaps they were planning on taking down the government.

Okay, so that wasn't likely to happen in North Carolina, but it would be easy to set such a story in Washington, DC, or even a city like Chicago or New York where the rich and powerful often visited. I'd argue those kinds of plot holes with myself for hours.

Done with putting away clothing, I picked my phone back up, intending to call my sister. Unfortunately, it said my battery was dead. I found my charger and plugged it in, puzzled. Normally my phone remained charged for quite some time. The weather wasn't so very cold, or even very hot, so the fact that the battery had just died, though I was certain it was more than half full when I'd come in from the car, was puzzling.

Still, you never knew. I went to the bathroom to explore that room. Again, it was larger than I expected.

The sink ran across from the door. A shower sat on the right and beside it was a toilet. On the left was a huge soaking tub with a raised stair that let you climb up and get into the tub easily. There were lights over the vanity and the sink but nowhere else, leaving both the shower and tub in a rather uninviting shadow. If I used the tub, I'd need candles, I decided.

Back in the room, I went to curl up on the sofa. It was weird that the television in this area was a flat screen against the wall that backed up to the bathroom and then the sofa went the long way. The recliner had its back to the bedroom, facing the television directly. There was more than enough space to have put the furniture the other way.

The wall over the sofa had an arrangement of photos. It was Kernroote Castle through the last hundred years. They were all in black and white. One had a carriage in front of the main doors, without the portico. Then there was another one from inside, when the place looked dark and shadowed in the gray-and-black coloring. There was a man standing near the door in an old-fashioned butler's uniform. The planes and angles of his face made him look like the man at the front desk.

They could be father and son, or perhaps grandfather and grandson, as I wasn't sure the last time someone had had a real butler. It was odd, though, to think that someone would still work here, having been a servant. Unless, of course, the servant had been left the place at some point in the past and now their family was running it. It would explain the change from private home to a boutique hotel that wasn't quite "boutique" by my definition.

I settled back on the sofa, making up stories about how this had happened until the day darkened into night. Even without lowering the room darkening shades, it was plenty dark. There were no streetlights and the night was just cloudy enough that there were few stars. The moon was a narrow crescent, either waxing or waning, I didn't know. I would soon enough when it got brighter or darker.

I turned back to the room and picked up my phone to call my sister. I couldn't wait to tell her about the oddness of the place. It would also make me feel better to hear another voice, to let me know I wasn't alone in the world. Unfortunately things were not be, because her phone rang and rang, eventually going to voice mail. I tried not to let it bother me. Kara lived across the country, but it did. I felt oddly lonely in the large place, like a child left alone too long late at night.

Chapter 3

The next morning I didn't feel particularly rested. It wasn't the bed, which was about as heavenly as can be. The thick white comforter had been perfectly luxurious and I had adjusted the thermostat to be a cool enough temperature that I could use it. It was the kind of bed you wanted to snuggle down in. I had loved crawling into it and enjoying the feel of the fine cotton sheets. The comforter even smelled new and fresh, leading me to believe that no one else had used this room. It was like moving into a brand-new home.

I had dropped off to sleep quickly enough. Unfortunately, I dreamed. First I dreamed fairly normal dreams, angry dreams telling off Daniel for leaving me. But then they turned to the castle. Instead of being black iron gates at the entrance, I had driven up to find skeletal arms blocking my way. In my dream, I knew that Kara was inside and I had to go in.

I dropped out of that dream and into one where I wandered the long, narrow hallway of my floor, exploring around the corners and finding rooms filled with junk and things that moved just out of the corner of my eye. I had dreamed I even woke in my room, but I wasn't alone. A shadowy figure had been in the corner near the French doors and stood watching me.

That had woken me up with a start. I didn't think I screamed but if I had, I was certain no one would have heard me. I turned on the lights around the room but the corner where my visitor had been remained dark. Returning from lighting all the lights, I couldn't help but notice the shadows looked like a shrouded figure.

The air conditioning purred quietly with the occasional rattle, like a sleeper with asthma or a cold suddenly needing air. I smelled the faintest smell of oranges although that wasn't anything I'd purchased at the store. I wondered where the scent came from or if it was a light perfume in the cleansers the hotel used to clean the rooms.

I left the lights on but crawled back into bed, where I drifted off again only to have more troubling dreams. This time I was running around the castle, from places that I had seen earlier in the day to places I had never been. At one point in my dream, I was taken down to the basement where the desk clerk insisted he show me something, which turned out to be the graveyard of his family, all buried beneath the castle. Wights sat about a table and I was there to be their next meal.

When I woke from that one, the sun was up in the sky, and I noted that I had slept for nearly ten hours, but it felt as if I'd slept not at all. I got up and dressed quickly so I could grab some of the breakfast included in the cost of the hotel. If I was paying for it, I didn't want to miss it.

As the night before, the hallway was silent. It seemed that in the morning the shadows were darker and longer than they had been the evening before. I shuddered, thinking about my dreams. I looked behind me and where

I had thought the hallway ended, it appeared that there was a corner rather than an end. I had no desire to go exploring just then, not after my dreams.

Once inside the silent elevator, which also smelled of oranges this morning, I rode down to the lobby area. The desk clerk wasn't around, again. Perhaps he was too busy haunting my dreams and the old photographs on my walls. I went out to the breakfast room.

A nice young woman was there and she let me sit where I wanted. There was an older couple in a corner with two windows. I picked a table not far from where they were, in case they were interested in being friendly, but not so close as to seem I was being overly intrusive. I was able to look out over the grounds.

Breakfast was either eggs scrambled with vegetables and feta cheese or there was a stuffed French toast. While the French toast was tempting, I needed to work, so I chose the eggs, which would offer a healthier fare. As I was ordering, the older couple got up and left the table.

I was sorry to see them go. I hadn't realized how lonely it felt in this huge place. The breakfast room should be stuffed with people, I thought. Instead it was now only me and one young woman server.

Although the waitress brought me tea and made a little bit of conversation, she didn't bring my breakfast. As I looked out the window, wondering if I should set myself up for writing or if I should go for a walk first, my eggs arrived, carried by a dark-eyed man.

"The scramble," he said, setting the plate down for me, which held a lovely pile of eggs, not too over-scrambled and filled with an assortment of vegetables and the white of feta cheese. Next to it sat two sausage links, an English muffin, a thick crock of butter and another of jam, along with fried potatoes and a sort of mini-Danish that looked filled with raspberry jam.

"It looks lovely I said.

He wasn't wearing an apron. Instead, he was just dressed in ordinary khaki slacks and a short sleeved, button-down shirt. Dark-haired, and with those eyes, he looked like he might play Heathcliff in an old movie.

"My chef is still learning, but I love my eggs this way. I had them like this out on the West Coast," he said.

"Your chef?" I asked. "Are you the owner, then?"

He smiled and nodded at that. "I am indeed. The lucky inheritor of Kernroote Castle and all the associated joys." His voice didn't hold the smile, and he seemed a bit annoyed that he was the one who inherited.

"But what a marvelous place. The rooms here are love-ly," I said.

"I'm glad you like it and I hope that you'll tell your friends."

"My sister is the one to tell people." Really, she was. Kara talked about everything—all her joys as well as her distresses. No doubt the people she worked with, as well as the friends she met just by being Kara, would all know about Kernroote, should I ever find a way to connect with her and tell her what I thought.

"Then I hope she'll join you while you're here. I noticed you've booked a rather long stay. Is it work related?"

"Sort of," I hedged. Was my writing actual work? I thought of it as finding myself. It was hard to think of myself as a writer rather than a middle manager, a busi-nesswoman, perhaps. I didn't have a clue about getting published, only that I had to have something written before I could publish anything.

Seeing my hesitation, my dark-eyed Heathcliff leaped

into the conversational gap, saying, "I'll leave you to your breakfast. It's best warm." He smiled and held my eyes a fraction longer than was necessary.

I didn't mind the look. I mean, he was handsome, seemed well-spoken, and clearly had money to invest in a hotel of sorts, even if it was an inheritance. Plus, it wasn't as if I was married any longer. Too bad I hadn't even gotten his name.

He was gone before I thought to ask, disappearing like a shadow in the bright daylight. Seeing he clearly wasn't going to keep me, I tucked into my eggs. As he had suggested, they were brilliant. Not too hard but cooked through. The cheese made them fluffier than eggs ordinarily were. I picked out spinach, tomatoes, onions, and mushrooms in the mix. I wondered if this was a regular meal of if there were other choices.

The rest of the food was equally exquisite and I wondered why they didn't have more patrons. Surely as people learned of this food, crowds would come here to eat. A brunch on Saturday or Sunday could be started. It seemed as if the place could use more people. I was sitting alone on a Friday morning. It could be that people only came up for a Saturday or Sunday excursion, but still. Perhaps tomorrow would be different.

Deep down I had a feeling it wouldn't be.

Chapter 4

After breakfast I went back to my room for a few moments before deciding to take a walk. Someone had already been there to clean the room, leaving everything as fresh as I could want. I had hardly had time to make my own mark on the place and I was erased just as quickly, except for the flotsam I carried with me. The place was lovely. It was unfortunate my thoughts were turning so dark, like the shadows in the corners.

Even so, I was feeling good after such a wonderful meal. I went back downstairs, using the French doors that led out to the terrace. I glanced back through the windows at the breakfast room and only the girl who had served me was there, washing off the tables as if looking for something to keep her occupied. I wondered if anyone else would be down.

She glanced up and I gave her a smile. She turned away without acknowledging it. Perhaps if someone trained the staff to be nicer there would be more guests. I was here for more than a month of this sort of treatment, I thought. Well, no matter. One must be nice if one hopes to get anything done.

I set off down the concrete steps. They were solid and looked as if they'd been there for ages. To either side of the wide steps was a railing for those who needed something to hang on to. I didn't notice a ramp of any sort but perhaps I was just missing it.

I skipped down the stairs, eager to get to the garden. On the ground, the garden was more mazelike than I had imagined. The bushes were taller than they seemed from the fifth floor, many raising over my head. Still, they were beautiful, despite the fact that most blooms were past their prime.

Faint sweet and tangy floral scents reached me but they weren't overwhelming. I found a patch of bright daylilies that had opened for the morning and reached towards the sun from their semi-shadowed spot. I paused to admire them. I didn't see a bench nearby so I had to stand and look. I continued to wander.

I wanted to see the pond, but the deeper into the garden I went, the taller the plants seemed to become. They were all nondescript plants with wide leaves that might have been evergreen. Below them, in the angles of the foliage, were shade-loving flowering plants of sorts I couldn't iden-tify. Instead of open areas where I could see parts of the path, I felt as if I were alone on a hiking trail. There were birds overhead but the cicadas were still silent in the morning air. I heard a frog croak once and then it stilled, as if in hiding. I wondered what it might be hiding from.

I walked through shaded rows, feeling the shadows get deeper, going so far as to keep the heat from the sun off my skin, though not blocking out the humidity. It was going to be a hot afternoon and uncomfortably humid. It surprised me that it would get that way even in the mountains. I thought it would stay somewhat cooler than down in Charlotte.

My mind wandered, thinking of Colorado, which would hold the dry air of the high desert. I would not miss the humidity at all. I came to a crossroads, or perhaps a cross path, looking around. I wasn't sure which way to go. One direction continued on into the shadows. The other three directions were brighter. I took the brighter path that seemed to go in a direction I wanted. Oddly, although paths sometimes crossed, they seemed to meander and curve so that it was hard to see very far ahead. Even the bright path had shadows waving, though I could feel no breeze on my skin.

The scent of the flowers receded and I thought I smelled a skunk, perhaps dead or defending itself, fortunately not too nearby. It got stronger as I continued on and I walked carefully through the too-silent garden. I never thought I'd be thankful for cicadas but I would have loved to have heard some just then.

I should have brought a compass or noticed where I was going. The garden didn't seem that large from my room, but as soon as I realized the plants were taller than I expected, I should have paid attention. But clearly I hadn't and now I was lost. I held down panic to the faint sweat on the palms of my hands. I could make my way out.

I kept going along this path, though the skunk smell was stronger here. There was nothing for it but to keep going. I came to a Y in the path, leaving me with two choices. I could veer off to the right or the left. To the left the shadows were darker, the flowers looked gray, and I thought that the stink of the skunk came from there.

I stayed right. The sun was hot coming down and I began to wonder how long I'd been wandering. It hadn't seemed all that long. Had I admired the daylilies for hours rather than minutes, like someone lost in fairyland? Still I kept walking. A large shadow passed overhead. I looked up but there was nothing there. Perhaps the angle of a hawk flying by had made it seem as if I were being stalked by a dragon.

I shuddered. I no longer liked the garden and wasn't surprised that no one else was wandering about. The flowers no longer looked beautiful, if a little off-season. They looked predatory and almost dead. The floral smell that would reach me now and again, over the skunk smell, seemed too sickly and too much, like an old woman's over-done perfume.

I hurried along, hoping to find an exit to the garden. I didn't care where I came out, knowing I could skirt the maze and stay close to the manor. I'd even go through the woods behind the place to walk around just to be out of the blasted maze.

The plants continued close together, hugging each other as if for comfort. They all reached over my head and there was no amount of poking through them to slip onto another path. I also had no way of knowing if such a thing would help.

My mouth felt dry and I wished I had brought some water. But who brings a bottle of water to walk through a garden? My heart rate was starting to speed up and I needed to calm down. Working myself up wasn't going to help me, not here in the maze.

I kept going. All the cross paths seemed to be dark and not very inviting. I finally took one, as the path I was on didn't seem to take me anywhere and I wasn't completely certain that I wasn't seeing the same paths over and over again. There was a low maple that hugged the ground, almost as if it were tired of life and had fallen over on its side, that made me think I'd been by that path before.

I started looking more closely. The next time a cross section of four paths intersected, I took the one on the left. I thought that it was the path I had come down. A few plants looked familiar but I couldn't be certain. As I wandered through the shadows, I felt chilled this time, though I continued to sweat and my tongue felt as it were stuck to the roof of my mouth.

The silence was broken by a rustling in the brush to my right. I paused, wondering what could be there. I heard the faintest growl and I moved quickly down the path, not certain what to do. If there were a beast in the garden, I was hopelessly lost with it.

The birds had stopped their songs, even the distant birds from away from the gardens. I heard nothing from the castle, but then I hadn't expected to. What I wouldn't give to have stayed at the hotel below the Biltmore watching crowds or perhaps walking around their safe gardens that weren't mazes without exits.

I came to another path that wound around to the right and this appeared to go straight. I couldn't remember which path I'd been on. Perhaps I should stay on one path, but what if this, too, just took me around in circles? I looked back at the shadowed area and I didn't like the look. Something gleamed between the leaves and while I told myself it was probably the angle of the sun on a bit of dew, I couldn't help think the eyes belonged to a monster, hidden all these years in the gardens.

I wanted to laugh at myself. Perhaps instead of trying to write romance, I should write horror. You'd think Stephen King were there with me, whispering ideas into my head while I walked the garden. I turned right.

This path was sunnier but there were patches of

shadow. If there was anything good about the path, it was that it seemed to be filled with less dense foliage. Perhaps I was nearly out. I heard the plink of water to my right and when the path curved, I was in the center of the garden, with the pond.

The pond wasn't as lovely up close. There was a musty smell to it, as if it wasn't properly cared for. There were no fish nor any fountain. In fact, there was a sprayer to keep the water circulating but it looked as if it hadn't been used in years. The plants were dead and many had rotted, which was likely the smell that I got. At least there weren't dead skunks here.

I turned away, disappointed, intending to wend my way back out of the garden, or try to.

I stopped short when the desk clerk appeared before me.

His eyes were as hooded as ever and the dark shadows that lurked behind the blackness of them pierced me with a disapproving stare. He wasn't pleased to find me in the garden. Perhaps it was his duty to trim the bushes as well.

"What are you doing here?" he asked.

I felt rather like Harry Potter being caught by Professor Snape. While the words had the slightest southern accent to them, the intonation was a perfect imitation of Alan Rickman's character in the movies.

"I was exploring the gardens," I said.

"Clearly." The Snape impression just got deeper, I thought.

I drew myself up. I was not a teenaged girl floundering around in her life. I was an adult woman who had paid good money to stay in a hotel. If there were gardens that were off limits, then there should be signs and clearly there had been no signs.

"I appear to have gotten myself a bit turned around

while I was exploring the gardens. While I had wanted to see the pond, I had thought it would be more pleasant," I explained.

I heard the faintest trickle of water behind me and then the croak of a frog. I turned to see that the pond wasn't the ugly, dead place I had thought. It was actually a living place with a frog and even a few fish. There was a large water lily that looked about ready to open the pink of its flower just visible around the green of the leaves that hadn't yet opened.

Overall, it was a pleasant place putting a lie to my words.

I looked back at the desk clerk. He looked at me a little sadly, perhaps because the place hadn't met my expectations. Later I would wonder if he understood what my seeing the dead and dying pond meant.

"Let me take you back to the castle then. You look overly warm," he said. Suddenly he was no longer a southern imitation of Professor Snape but rather a Southern gentleman who worked in the service industry doing his best to offer assistance to a customer.

"Thank you," I said. It was a perplexing turn.

We wended our way through the garden, which was furiously simple. A child could have done it. The plants that had seemed so tightly packed, almost overgrown were clearly just planted in clumps. The floral scents were no longer the sort that an old woman wore but rather ones you expected in the garden. Even the daylilies I had admired waved as I passed.

We were just coming out of the entrance when I was confronted with the owner.

"Zachary," the desk clerk said with the slightest incline of his head.

Zachary was clearly surprised to see me following his

desk clerk. "Lost in the garden?" he asked. His voice was friendly rather than disapproving. The desk clerk moved off and towards the castle.

"A bit," I said. "Fortunately someone came to my rescue."

"What did you think of our gardens? Other than they have a tendency to be a bit wilder than they appear from above?"

"Quite lovely," I said. I wasn't certain why I felt a need to be somewhat circumspect with him.

But my comments just made him let out a breath and smile in relief. "I've had complaints of a smell in there, though no one has ever been able to find it. I hate it when things don't meet the guest's expectations."

"Certainly it's a lot to take on," I said. I wanted to ask him all sorts of questions about the place, about why it was so silent.

His eyes held mine and we looked at each other for a long moment, while I struggled to find a tactful way to ask my questions and he appeared to struggle for something to say, anything at all.

"I should leave you to your wanderings then," he said.

"I think I've had enough wandering," I replied. "I thought I'd head back to my room and do a bit of work."

Zachary led me up the concrete steps and held open the door to the building. I entered, turning to thank him, but he was already looking off at the garden, frowning.

"I will see you later then," he said, turning back to me, the smile coming quickly.

I watched for a moment as he headed pensively towards the gardens. He looked like a man worried about something and I felt for him. I turned away and walked through the main entry area and around the desk. Wherever the clerk had gone, it had not been to the desk.

I rounded the corner and saw a figure, tall and broad, hurry into the elevator and push the button. The doors closed before I could stop them and he appeared to glare at me, gray eyes beneath pale lids that felt like a chilly, cloudy day, when he spotted me. I could do nothing but wait.

Chapter 5

I attempted to start writing. In fact, I did start writing four or five times. And then I deleted everything. It was as if the story that I'd been mentally writing for years didn't have a start or a way in. I didn't know what I wanted to write.

I had dreamed of being a romance writer, writing about the cute and wonderful fated meeting and then the story where the world tries to hold the lovers apart, the two of them overcoming everything. Instead, I kept starting out with a dark, scary setting that didn't fit the idea I had always held in my mind. It was as if the shadows of the garden were keeping me from seeing the story I knew I had inside me.

I picked up my phone, thinking I might call my sister. I was surprised to see I had a message from her. I listened to it. I checked my settings, but my phone was set to ring and there were no Do Not Disturb settings turned on.

I tried to call her back but only got her voicemail again. I sighed. It just wasn't my day.

I paced around the room, but decided it would be good

to get out and about. The writing wasn't going well at all. Maybe a more normal setting would help. I had shuddered when I'd noticed that according to the clock, I'd spent over two hours in the garden. Perhaps a normal run into town would reset my time sense.

I grabbed my purse and my keys and took the elevator down to the lobby. As usual, no one was at the desk. The man who stood outside, under the portico, was pulling a few weeds from the front of the hotel. He didn't turn when I came out, so I didn't go out of my way to greet him.

I got in my car and drove out of the parking lot, going slowly so as not to send gravel flying and potentially hurt the poor man who was clearly a jack of all trades.

I noticed there were only two cars there that day. Of course, it was the middle of the day, so perhaps people were out and about. I glanced up in the rearview mirror to see the uniformed man glaring at me. Perhaps it was only the angle of the sun and he was merely staring at my car. Still, it gave me a shiver. I'd done nothing but attempt to be nice to him.

I'd go towards Asheville and find some nice place to eat lunch. Maybe Kara would call me and we'd chat and I'd feel normal again. I hated to admit how weird I continued to feel about the incident in the garden.

I hadn't felt as if much time had passed but clearly it had. And then seeing the dead pond but having it change to something else almost immediately after made me shiver. I had no idea what was going on, but it made sent a chill up my spine so strong that I could feel my hair standing on end. Out on the road leaving the place, I decided I disliked everything about the castle. Well, except perhaps the comfortable bed.

The day was a perfect day for a drive. Although it was late summer and a Friday, it was still early enough that traffic wasn't horrible until I got closer to town. Things started to get more congested, but I saw signs for familiar restaurants and suddenly I wanted something familiar. While it was nice to experiment, I wanted something normal.

I took the first exit with a restaurant that promised large and familiar burgers. They were a family place and while it wasn't a weekend, I was pleased that upon walking in, there were a lot of people there with families. Kids were laughing and talking in the background and adults talked and argued. The music was turned up so that the waitress had to speak loudly over the din.

It was just what I needed after the too-silent hotel. I had a seat in a small booth made for two and quickly ordered a large lunch. I knew that the hotel served dinner but I wasn't sure I was up to silent dining so I ate well. This might be the only meal I got.

The smells of French fries and fish and garlic and frying meat melded into one big sensory overload which, instead of shutting me down, made my senses bloom. When I finished, I walked outside to the hot summer sunshine, the sound of traffic racing back and forth, the occasional honk of a horn and the smells of exhaust, rancid oil, and more French fries.

I could go back to the hotel and write or I could walk around and take in more stimulation. This wasn't a good place to walk—a restaurant row with few opportunities for seeing anything—so I reluctantly got back in the car. I had no real desire to do anything much. It was too hot to walk around outside. I considered looking for a mall to wander in but didn't want to waste my time. I had only a few months to write my book. Wasn't that what I came for?

So with a level of reluctance that surprised me, I drove back to the hotel. The highway west held cars. Even the turnoff held traffic enough to keep me company as I drove. I noticed I'd passed a couple of restaurants near the on-ramp, which could have interested me if I'd not been so hell-bent on finding a lot of people. The turnoff to the hotel and the black iron gates, perpetually open and perhaps welcoming in another era, came more quickly than I anticipated. I slowed and made the turn without causing an accident.

Quickly enough the traffic noises faded and I was alone on the road to the hotel. It was me and my radio. I looked at my phone, wishing my sister would call. Probably hadn't gotten my message or perhaps she was working again. There was the time difference, too. Between her shift work and the difference in hours I could never plan on when I'd hear from her, although I knew she'd be waiting to hear about my time at the hotel.

I made the curve and the castle appeared before me, almost as breathtaking as yesterday, though today instead of a regal place, I saw a large conglomerate of shapes and shadows. Was that moss on the roof nearest the car? What about the dark places on the stones along the walls? They no longer looked so pristine.

I sighed. It was probably my mood. Certainly the shining sun versus the setting sun would create different shadows. Just because I thought I saw someone looking out of a window on the fourth floor didn't mean that there wasn't a guest there. After all, there were now three cars in the parking lot.

If I were there, I might be looking out at the parking lot, hoping to see someone. In another week, if the silence kept up, I might be waving frantically like a madwoman trapped in an attic.

By the time I parked, the curtain had fallen and there wasn't a sign that anyone was there. Just another guest. I looked up at the building, searching to see if I could make out the sixth and seventh floors. Yes, I had missed the dormer windows on the sixth floor and there were small ones above that, but they had looked like vents from where I stood. I recounted and there were indeed seven floors above ground and clearly a basement, as the building had the ramp going up from the ground.

The-white uniformed man stood near the portico. He nodded at me but didn't smile. I nodded back.

Inside, there was no one in the entry area. The silence dragged out, like a huge, oversized, empty house. I went to the elevator and pressed the button for five.

I considered pressing six or seven just to see what those places looked like but decided if I were here, I should write.

At my room, I turned on my MP3 player and sat in front of my computer. I typed away without any enthusiasm until the shadows got longer, and the from way the lamplight met the curtain, I was beginning to feel as if the shadows were reaching towards me, about to grab my arm.

I got up to turn on the lights and look out at the balcony. I could go sit out there and look down at the garden. Perhaps I would feel more enthusiastic about writing there. I went in and got my computer and sat outside. I turned off my music and listened to the birds and even the cicadas who sounded more distant than they should have.

I didn't hear the frogs that I'd heard near the pond. The air was still hot and stifling, and the sun fell directly on me. I lasted all of a half an hour and that was pure stubbornness. I got up to go inside but paused at the door. The shadows felt wrong and I had no desire to enter the room.

No doubt I was being fanciful. My romance was taking a dark turn with my lovers having to confront the deaths of people close to them. Perhaps that was on my mind. It was this place. No doubt with its age, it had seen a lot of death. Perhaps I was just picking up the mood of sorrow the building felt.

I pushed open the French doors and went into the cool room. I felt the brush of the air-conditioned breeze against my sweaty skin and breathed in deeply. The room was starting to smell like me, rather than like a sterile hotel room. It was both a good experience and an odd one.

I looked around at the shadows in the corners, but they were where they were supposed to be and not moving around at all. Clearly my sense of dread was just my imagination. I was a little let down by the fact that the ghosts I had thought haunted the place didn't actually haunt it.

My phone rang and startled me. I rushed to get it. Kara, finally, calling me back.

Chapter 6

"So how is it?" Kara's voice was grainy and it sounded as if we were talking from a great distance. I guess that was true enough but I wasn't used to having it sound like that. My cell provider usually had better reception than that.

"It's nice enough," I said. There must have been a hesitation in my voice because she immediately jumped back in.

"What is it?"

"It's just weird. Too quiet, I guess." I settled back in the chair but then the phone went silent. I waited for Kara to answer but nothing.

I looked at the phone. No connection.

I sat forward and dialed Kara again.

"Phone breaking up?" she asked.

"I sat back in the chair," I said.

"So this way even I can't interrupt you as you write."

"I got a little done this afternoon, but I'm not sure it's any good. It's not the story I want to tell. I guess it's this creepy old place. Everything is getting so dark. I keep writing stuff about death."

Kara listened as I described the garden and getting lost. I didn't tell her about the dead pond turned living pond. That was clearly my imagination.

"Sounds like that hotel in *The Shining*, almost."

I laughed a little, not liking her comparison. "Hey, I'm here for a long time, so stop that. I'll freak myself out. At least the bed's comfortable."

"Well, see!" Kara was thrilled at that.

I thought about telling her about Zachary, the owner. He did seem like a nice guy, but I was curiously unwilling to comment about him. Normally I told Kara everything, but this didn't seem like something I should be talking about. It occurred to me that I didn't want to talk about it on the grounds, as if Kernroote was listening to me.

I made a face, though there was no one to see it, and went back to talking to Kara.

When I hung up, I felt both better and lonelier. This would be an amazing place to explore if I had a friend or my sister or to explore with me.

I sighed and tried to get back to writing. What I ended up doing was deleting everything I had written. I didn't want to write about dead families and family secrets. I wanted to write about weddings and joy and perhaps the simple things that kept people apart for no good reason. I just couldn't seem to make that happen. Perhaps going through a painful divorce wasn't the best time to contemplate writing a happy romance.

With that thought, I went downstairs. In the lobby, I looked out at the breakfast room. No one was around. While I had read, and certainly smelled, that there was a restaurant, I didn't know exactly where it was. As I stood there, considering my options, I heard people come in through the front door.

I turned, thrilled to see that there was a party of six people, three men and three women, coming in to the hotel. The uniformed man had a trolley with suitcases, but two of the men also pulled large pieces of luggage. The women were giggling together, looking at the ceiling.

"We'll be through in time for an early dinner, won't we? I've heard good things about the restaurant," the oldest of the men said. They all had gray hair at the sides of their head but this man was all gray. His face was more lined than the others' as well. All of the women looked my age or younger, so clearly they weren't contemporaries of them.

I felt disappointed in the people, although no doubt it was common enough.

"Not a problem," the uniformed man said.

The desk clerk appeared from somewhere in the shadows. He looked at everyone with his typical disapproving glance and then asked, "Who shall go first?"

"I will," the older man said. "Reservation for Barron. Jackson Barron the Third." He said it as if everyone should have heard of him. I hadn't. But I decided now was as good of a time as any to ascend to the second floor. Perhaps the dining room was there.

I walked around the catwalk that looked down on the first floor. I heard a faint sound from my right, so I turned that way and went down a narrow corridor that led to a glass door with the sign that said, "Kernroote Fine Dining." I opened the door only to have to turn down a hall that led back the way I had come until I got to sign that asked me to wait to be seated.

I did so. Soon enough, a young man came up and

asked how many were in my party. He looked disappointed when I said just one.

"Are you staying here?" he asked.

I nodded.

He smiled at me. "Seen any ghosts?"

I shook my head, smiling. Surely he was joking.

"We all joke about it, but this place is weird. We give ten percent off if you have a good ghost story. We don't tell people until after we've asked, but now you'll know for next time, right?"

"Right." I smiled.

I wondered what he'd think of my garden story. Was that really a ghost story or just a creepy tale of imagination gone wild?

He settled me down in a booth that was near a window. I could look out over the setting sun and the garden. They had filtered shades that kept the sun from being too bright but still let you see out at the landscape. Everything about the restaurant was elegant, from the deep red carpet, which was as plush as everywhere else, to the dark black-leather booths.

There was soft music playing in here, which soothed me, even if it was an unrecognizable violin piece. At least it was sound. There were four other couples in the restaurant, mostly seated in booths near the window, although one sat on the far side by what looked to be a bar, complete with the mirror behind it and a selection of alcohol.

The wood, like all the wood, was mahogany. If you pulled the wood out of the place, you'd probably be able to make a fortune. Given how few people I'd seen, perhaps that would be a better use of the funds that could come from Kernroote than trying to make it a hotel.

I began to wonder how they were doing their advertising or if they really wanted more people. Maybe they liked it quiet. Maybe they weren't quite ready for a grand opening.

I read the menu, which was done in a fake red leather with gold lettering on the front. Inside was a page that appeared handwritten on parchment, complete with the slightly burnt edges, held in place by the menu cover's corner holders. It was a nice touch. There were things like that scattered about the hotel that almost made me glad to be staying there.

It was clearly a place for fine dining. I smelled cooking food, probably beef. I worked to dismiss my fancies from earlier about what sort of meat might be cooking here. My stomach needed no such urging as it rumbled, despite the huge lunch I'd had earlier.

The menu was spare, offering three different steaks, a vegetarian dish that looked like a stuffed Portobello mushroom, a duck dish, and an elk dish. I tried to think what sounded good but everything sounded odd and strange, much like the castle itself. Now would be a fine time to talk to someone about the options and what might be good. I mean, creamed leeks? Who ate leeks and who, particularly, ate them creamed?

And the appetizers. Tuna tartar? Was that really raw tuna? Was that like sushi or sashimi, which I was much more familiar with than tuna tartar? Could they at least say something like that?

I shook my head. The duck sounded good. I was tempted by the elk, but wasn't sure how rich or filling it would be. And I'd had beef earlier so I wanted something different. The duck sounded different enough and when my waiter came, an older gentleman with the bluest eyes I'd ever seen, stopped by to take my drink order, I was ready to order my meal as well as a drink.

I ordered a glass of the house wine, red, because he

said the duck was a rich enough dish to order red. So I did. The one at his recommendation. The prices in the restaurant were higher than I'd have liked. I wouldn't be eating there regularly, but it was Friday and this was a treat.

A group of three women, clearly coming in from work, walked pointedly towards the bar. The maître d' clearly knew them and let them go. Apparently the restaurant did bring in some business. I found that pleased me. It was too bad the restaurant was set off to itself so that you'd never know it was there from the main entrance.

It might have been done on purpose, in case things got busy at the castle. People waiting to check in wouldn't have to put up with people waiting for tables. Still, it seemed a strange way to lay things out.

I watched as one of the women tossed her head, her blown-out dark hair swinging around so that it nearly hit her friend, which sent them all into peals of laughter. They were wearing tank tops and nice slacks. All it would have taken was a blazer or a sweater over the top to make it a perfect business outfit. The black pumps, not too high on the heel, told me I was right about them having an after-work girls' night.

My wine came and the waiter stood by while I tasted it. When I nodded at him, he smiled. Not that I knew what I was looking for when I tasted it, but clearly it was something to drink.

The shades that dimmed the setting sun, and the dark wood and soft lighting, added more shadows than I'd have appreciated elsewhere in the building. Here the people and the soft music took the edge off of those same shadows. So what if there was a shadow that looked as if it was caressing the straight-haired brunette's shoulder like a lover? She hadn't noticed and was having fun.

The couple who sat nearest me had a shadowy third.

The slightest movement from around the restaurant made the shadow move towards a plate like someone trying to steal treats. It was more mischievous than frightening. It even brought a smile to my lips. I tried to see where the shadow was coming from but even though I couldn't point to one thing, I didn't let it worry me. I was in a place with other people. I had company surrounding me and I was safe.

I sipped away at my wine.

When the duck came, I signaled the waiter for another glass. I picked away at the foods, most of which I didn't recognize. Fortunately there were no creamed leeks, but there was a strange sort of root vegetable and something green and bitter, but surprisingly tasty. It complimented the duck sauce, which was faintly sweet.

I settled back, eating slowly, looking out the window. It was too dark to read easily, even if I had remembered my e-reader but that was okay. I tried to play with my phone but there wasn't a signal here. Probably not much coverage, which explained the poor connection I had with Kara earlier.

The wine relaxed me. Even when the people nearby got up and the shadow followed them, I didn't react. I just watched, interested rather than frightened. I was nearly done with the duck when Zachary appeared. He was dressed in a black tuxedo that fit him perfectly. Clearly there was more to his inheritance than just the castle.

He looked around the room, which quieted slightly at his appearance. I watched him and the patrons out of the corner of my eye. I had the perfect place near the entrance, slightly hidden by the maître d's corner. The women at the bar turned to look, giggling again. One looked as though she was trying to catch his eye. Apparently this was a regular thing, then. He was probably meeting those women, his friends.

His eyes seemed to pass over them, not noticing them. But me—when he saw me, his eyes widened fractionally and he strode purposefully across the short distance to my booth.

"I see you've found our restaurant. I trust the food is to your liking?"

"It's quite good," I said.

He nodded. "And breakfast?"

"Also lovely. Do you have the scramble every morning?"

"If you wish, we can make up anything you like," he told me.

I nodded. "I just wondered what sorts of things I'll have to look forward to."

He smiled, his eyes not leaving mine. I felt a nice warm tingle in my lower belly. I wished I could flirt more easily. Normally when I write romance scenes in my head, words flow easily and flirting comes naturally, the hero and heroine speaking in pithy phrases designed to delight. Now I just felt tongue-tied, not wanting him to leave but not knowing what to say.

"It was lovely seeing your gardens earlier, even if they are a bit easy to get lost in," I said.

A shadow seemed to flit behind his eyes, but Zachary held the smile. "It's always nicest to see them with company. Should you wish, I would be happy to give you a tour. Tomorrow? Unless, of course, you have other plans?"

"Not at all," I said. "I'm here basically to work."

"Such a slave driver your boss must be to expect you to work on the weekend."

"Oh, it's not that," I said suddenly embarrassed. My cheeks were warm from the wine and embarrassment. I felt like he could sense the ache I felt for him. Was it wishful thinking on my part or did he lean forward slightly as if he wanted to be closer to me, to find a way to touch?

"Really?" His voice was lower. I felt the warmth of his breath near my ear.

"I'm just trying to write a book. I figured a place like this, I could be inspired."

Zachary leaned back, much to my disappointment, and looked at me. "I have to say I'm not sure I saw you as the sort of person to be inspired by Kernroote. You look far too nice to be trying to imitate Stephen King." There was a smile.

I lifted my hand as if to wave that off, even as I laughed a little. He reached out to take it.

"I only know you as Ms. Winter in room five-thirty-five. I'm sure you must have a first name. I'll have to have it to find the book when it comes out."

"Everyone calls me Becca," I said quietly.

He let go of my hand, which now felt too cold, though electric fire was still singing through it, and nodded at me again.

"I have duties to see to and you have dinner to finish. It seems I'm always interrupting your meals, which is not my intent."

"It's not interruption. It's quite nice to have someone to chat with for a few moments."

"Then I shall endeavor to make your stay more enjoyable. Tomorrow morning around ten-thirty for the tour?"

"I'll look forward to it," I said.

I watched him walk around the room, glad-handing the others in much the same way he had me, though he never stayed near anyone quite so long. Several times he glanced over at my table, a hesitant look upon his face, then a smile. Finally he reached the bar. One of the women there reached up and gave him a long hug.

Much too long from where I sat. She leaned forward as if she were going to kiss him, but I missed that when my waiter came to ask if I was finished. I looked down at my plate, which was empty. Clearly I was.

"Yes, thank you." I said.

"Dessert?" he asked.

I had thought about it earlier. Considered having some just to be there again should Zachary make another round of the room, but he was with the women, who were clearly businesswomen who came in often. Perhaps the one was even dating him.

"That's all, thank you," I said.

"Very good." He turned away, taking my plate. I swirled what was left in my wine glass and watched the red coloring move back and forth like blood spatter.

The man from the elevator, who had seemed so annoyed by my trying to share with him, passed by my table. He turned to give me a look, perhaps surprise at seeing me again, but I avoided his eyes. I noticed the slight curl of his light brown hair, an unkempt look so different from Zachary's. I was nearly done with my meal and busy trying to decide why I disliked seeing Zachary with the businesswoman at the bar, so I avoided his gaze.

As soon as the check came, I signed it and then went back to my room to start my book afresh.

Chapter 7

I got back to my room and settled in to write. I worked for nearly an hour, writing out a meet-cute with plenty of lustful looks and words. It wasn't quite what I had hoped, but there didn't seem to be any deaths coming anytime soon. I had a mental outline for the book I wanted to write, so I decided to put that down on paper, to get my brain excited about it and to exorcise the ghosts that seemed to want to filter into my novel.

When I finished, it was full dark and the room was filled with shadows. The building was, as usual, silent. I sighed. I was pleasantly relaxed, though, and decided not to let anything worry me. I went out on the balcony, hoping to hear other people talking outside. I wasn't intending to eavesdrop on anyone, but I wanted to hear voices murmuring, perhaps smell a bit of cigarette smoke, hear movement on gravel, just anything to remind I wasn't alone in the castle.

Instead I heard only the song of frogs and perhaps a car in the front. I almost wished my room overlooked the parking lot. Then I could be the shadow woman looking out her window at the people coming and going. I smiled to myself. I looked around at the hotel windows on the back side, hoping to see a light on in a room somewhere. There was one to the right on the second floor. I couldn't see anything right below me, but it gave me hope that there were more lights that I just couldn't see.

I turned to go in, but felt a chill against my shoulder. There wasn't a breeze but it was as if I had suddenly put a cold pack on my shoulder. It was a strange sensation that lifted as soon as I turned my head. The shadows were moving around the building, like tree branches waving in the wind, but there was nothing to throw shadows around. And there was no breeze at all.

My contented mood quickly evaporating, I went inside.

I decided I needed a shower, perhaps to wash off the chill feeling that still echoed in my shoulder. I'd be fresh for the morning after that lovely bed.

The shower, while large enough for two, was so dark it was hard to see anything. Shadows played around me and I found myself trying to avoid stepping in the places that were covered in them. I didn't know why exactly. It wasn't as if they were going to attack. At least, I didn't really think so. My active imagination might have other comments.

I shampooed my hair, washed the rest of me, and got out of there as quickly as possible. Perhaps the poor lighting was a way to keep people from using too much water? Maybe tomorrow I'd try the deep soaking tub. I realized I could have purchased some candles when I was in town. I'd have to consider that in the next few days. The tub was much too dark, and the idea of having the shadows flowing around me with the water made me want to run from the room.

I felt stupid thinking that and stubbornly made myself stand there and dry my hair. The task done, I settled onto the very comfortable bed to watch some television, hoping that the mundane act of mindless TV would drive away the strange thoughts I'd been having.

Television didn't help. It made noise, which felt oddly out of place in the silence of the room. Listening to music through my earbuds didn't have the same odd effect. It was as if something were listening and didn't like the sound of the TV. No shows caught my attention and I kept glancing into the corners to see if the shadows had moved closer to the bed.

Rather than freak myself out even more, I turned off the television, left the lights on, and snuggled under the covers. Fortunately the mattress was as comfy tonight as it had been the night before and I fell asleep easily. My dreams this time were more pleasant, of meeting Zachary and going for a drive in an old car. While there were a few times when I felt uncomfortable, looking over my shoulder to see the desk clerk staring at me, overall I when I woke, I woke happy and refreshed and not at all frightened or scared.

In fact, I practically bounced out of bed though it was still early. I sat down to work on my romance novel. I spent about an hour typing away, lost in a pleasant dream where Zachary had taken me to lunch after our walk and then we'd talked all afternoon. I shouldn't let my mind run ahead from what was going on, based on nothing more than a few flirtatious glances, but it helped my creative mind so it seemed rather harmless.

I finished a good three pages before I looked up and noticed the time. I needed to get ready for breakfast and a walk. I dressed with a little more care, taking some time for makeup and doing my hair. I wore my most flattering set of capris, my favorite blue top, and walking sandals. I wanted to be able to walk but not look like I planned a hike, as I had yesterday. This time I wanted to show myself off to my best effect.

My hair tended to be unruly and although I used the flat iron, I noticed that it still wanted to gap at my part. I worked a little harder so that it became a long waterfall of red-brown hair glowing under the bathroom lights. The eyeliner brought out the highlights in my brown eyes, making them look almost hazel. It also softened the some-times too-pink color of my cheeks, particularly seeing I had gotten a bit more sun than I had wanted yesterday.

Satisfied that I looked as good as I was going to, I grabbed my key and headed down to breakfast. The hotel was still too silent. I appeared to be the only one on the fifth floor. I wondered why my room was so far down the hall if no one else was on the floor. I had a momentary temptation to head left to see what was down the wing I had run through in my dream from a few nights ago, but I put that off. Another time, perhaps after my walk.

Once in the elevator, I expected a smooth ride to the first floor. Instead it stopped at the third floor. I smiled then, expecting someone to get on with me, but although the elevator waited there for a few moments, no one else got on. I didn't expect the disappointment that came with the silent closing of the doors, leaving me, once again, alone. Normally I couldn't care less if I was in an elevator alone. After all, you had more room, but the hotel was getting to me with its silence and lack of people.

I got off at the lobby, flicking a glance over at the desk. I started when I noticed the desk clerk working, head down, looking at something below my line of sight. He glanced up as I jumped but he didn't give me any sort of reaction or even a "Good morning," which would have been polite. Instead he just looked back down as if I didn't exist at all.

There were two older women in the breakfast room this morning and a man and a woman about my age. One couple was at one end and one at the other. I chose the end closest to the two women not because of any preference, but because it was further from the French doors and I didn't want to feel the heat if anyone went in and out, although given the lack of people around that seemed unlikely.

A different young girl from yesterday, this one with red hair and freckles, asked me for my order, offering the choices today. I could get an omelet stuffed with crab, mushrooms, scallions, and spinach topped with hollandaise sauce or I could have a pancakes and my choice of peach or blueberry compote on the top. I ordered the omelet.

I watched the young woman leave, taking a sip of my water. I hoped that Zachary was around. However, my breakfast was brought to me by the young woman, her red hair, pulled back in a safe ponytail jiggling around trying to escape its holder.

While the food was delicious, I couldn't help but feel a little disappointed. I had such hopes that perhaps Zachary would come out with my food once again and join me while I ate. When I finished, I still had half an hour before we were due to meet. I could stay downstairs and play on my phone or I could go back upstairs.

I didn't want to appear too eager for a meeting so I rode the elevator up in solitary silence. Really, I began to wonder, how expensive could it be to install some sort of sound system?

I got off the elevator at my floor and the narrow hallway beckoned rather gloomily. I walked down the hall, considered stopping at my door, but continued on past, wanting to take a walk around the hotel and see if there was anything interesting. And to see how similar it was to my dream.

I walked the distance to where the hallway curved, noting that there was a room on the far end that looked quite a bit larger than the one I was in and turned. The green-and-gray carpet continued along the hall. The walls seemed darker although it may have been lower lighting. Down this part of the hallway there were old fluorescent lights beneath yellowed plastic, and their slight buzz made the hallway feel crowded and noisy.

I walked down this hallway, looking at doors. Most of them had numbers, but these had two fives in front of the room number, 5510 and so on. I wondered why that was. Perhaps to let the front desk know approximately where the room was, but you'd think they would have a map for that.

One of the doors was open slightly and I looked inside. The floor was covered in carpet, which had plastic over the top. The walls were stripped to the wallboard and hadn't been painted. There was no furniture in there, just an old ladder and a bucket, as if someone had been working. My nose twitched at the overpowering scent of paint when I got too close to the room.

I backed away. I hated that they really were finishing this area. I wondered if there were certain areas that were finished and others that weren't. It was certainly possible that I was the first person to use my room. I finished my walk down to the end of the hall. I could have run my fingers along the walls quite easily but when I reached out, the walls felt slimy against my fingers, so I avoided touching them. What a strange place.

The end of the hall offered a stairwell and I knew I could use it but I turned back, planning to go back to the elevator. I was disappointed that the end of the hall offered no window where I could look outside. The lights flickered and the shadows danced around. I was reminded of the dreams and of the sense that the shadows were more than just than they seemed.

I turned and hurried back along the narrow corridor. The fluorescent light outside the room with the door ajar chose that moment to flicker off for a prolonged period of time, plunging me into half-darkness. Now I was in shadow instead of avoiding it.

The hallway took on a new look, the carpet worn and old, nearly bare in spots. It no longer looked green but appeared a deep blue, almost black. The walls were narrow and paneled from floor to ceiling in the dark mahogany wood. A few pictures hung along the walls. I paused at one to look more closely at it. Skeletal branches of a huge tree reached out towards the sunshine, as if grasping for the sunlight to pull it into itself. It was only as I was looking that I saw the faces in each of the branches. The hairs on the back of my neck stood up. Something was very wrong. I shuddered and hurried along strange corridor.

I barely blinked and I was through the darkened corridor and back in the hall I knew, the narrow one that smelled of nothing at all and echoed only with the buzzing sounds of fluorescent lights. I looked back but the light behind me was on and the carpet was the green and gray and looked every bit as plush as the part I stood on.

I hurried around the corner, safely back to my normal hallway where the lights were a little bright. Still the shadows now seemed longer. I checked my phone but I didn't have time to go to my room. The walk had taken me nearly twenty-five minutes, rather than the five I thought it would. I hurried back to the elevator.

I didn't push the button so much as punch it. While I found the whole old hallway and new hallway business creepy enough to leave me feeling chilled, it was the fact that I had lost nearly twenty minutes that bothered me. It was like the garden, when I thought I had wandered for just a few minutes but it had been much, much longer.

The elevator arrived. Having no wait for the elevator was one nice thing about the place being nearly empty. And they were smooth and silent. I considered asking to have my room changed to something closer to the thing but decided against that. I didn't want to face the disapproving desk clerk.

I was relieved to see that when I arrived back down at the lobby that Zachary wasn't there yet. I wandered over to the door to go out onto the back patio. The day was a bit cloudier than yesterday, almost as if it was promising rain. Still, it wasn't raining yet, and I didn't see any black clouds coming in suggesting I'd get soaked any time soon. Zachary wasn't around so I sat on the steps, wishing they'd had chairs of some sort so people could enjoy the patio.

I had sat there nearly ten minutes when the man with the gray eyes from the elevator came out through the French doors from the breakfast room. He nodded at me. I gave him a small smile.

"It looks like a nice day, doesn't it?" he said. He was dressed in shorts and tennis shoes. His nose looked a little too small for his face. He had pale skin that probably burned easily, which was probably why he was out walking so early.

"It does," I agreed pleasantly.

He appeared about to say more but Zachary chose that moment to rush through the side door I'd used.

"I'm sorry. I got sidetracked by the accounts," he said. He held out a hand to me, helping me stand. "I'm definitely ready for a quiet walk. How about you?"

"It sounds marvelous," I replied, smiling.

The gray-eyed man nodded and slipped back inside, leaving us alone.

Zachary made a point of being obvious about taking in my outfit, and it was clear from the slight widening of his eyes that he approved, although he said nothing. He didn't let go of my hand until, at the bottom of the stairs, he seemed to realize what he was doing and pulled away as if embarrassed.

"The garden has been part of the estate for as long as anyone remembers. There are books about how the estate grew, but this and the main part of the castle, the part we've already renovated rather than the wings, have been here forever," Zachary said as he led me to the entrance of the garden.

The birds twittered, and off in the distance, cicadas played their tunes. I heard the frog that lived in the pond. There was also the familiar scuff of gravel beneath out feet as we walked towards the garden.

"How old is the castle?" I asked.

Zachary shrugged. "Well over two hundred years old. I have diaries of some ancestors that go back that far, and in the will it said I had to keep on the Perlette family, who had been with them since the 'beginning.' I was forbidden from ever selling the property. I could leave it to fall into disrepair but I can't ever sell the thing. If I had had brothers or sisters, one of us could have bought out the others, but our children would still be potential heirs."

"How fascinating." I was thinking about what a strange place this was as we passed into the early gardens where the low bushes came up to my knees and the taller trees were widely spaced. Zachary turned to the left rather than the right that I had gone. Perhaps this was the answer to the maze that had confused me.

There were splashes of low perennial flowers in pinks

and whites falling near the ground, with larger, heavily greened bushes and some bluish-colored grasses surrounding them. A few steps and we were standing near an old ornamental maple tree, probably a Japanese maple that must be decades old as it stood nearly as tall as I was, though it had the familiar bent-over pattern, shading some green and white hostas with their wide, corn-shaped leaves.

The fertile earth here smelled of damp and flowers and made me want to be a gardener. The sun went behind a cloud, leaving us in the shadow of the tree, but while I was a bit chilled, there was nothing odd about the shadows, not here, not with Zachary. I even heard the way the gravel moved as he bent to look more closely at one of the hostas.

"Hostas are my favorites because in the summer their leaves get so wide and they cover ground. I used to like to hide things here and then later on I'd go searching, just to see if I could find the toy I had left again," Zachary said.

I had nothing to say, thinking what large gardens these must be that a child could forget where they'd hidden a toy.

"You probably think I'm crazy," he said, mistaking my silence for judgment. "But the gardens can be strange sometimes. I used to think I saw things that weren't here, but I had a good imagination as a child."

"I'm a writer so I don't think you have to worry about me making judgments about that," I said, seeing he looked so embarrassed at the admission.

He gave me a rather sheepish smile and stood so we could return to the walk.

"I used to love running around in here. My mother hated it, of course. Because, while this isn't a maze, it can be surprisingly hard to find someone in here. It's like the sounds echo in the wrong places." Our shoes continued to crunch but I no longer heard the cicadas.

"It did seem unusually quiet in here yesterday," I admitted. I wasn't going to tell him what I had seen though. That was just crazy.

Zachary nodded. "I've never quite been able to figure out what does it. You'd think surrounded by the walls, it would create a sort of chamber and things would be louder, but it doesn't work that way."

I never considered that, although to be honest I was no sound technician. I had a hard time adjusting the volume on my television without Daniel's help. The picture I could deal with, but the sound…for some reason the sound perplexed me.

The birds were silent except for the scream of a distant hawk. It was probably hunting far away. I didn't hear the frog, either, but the lack of its voice didn't bother me while I was with Zachary. I heard the gravel beneath our feet. And once, I heard a woman's soft laughter.

I know I looked surprised, and surprise crossed Zachary's face as well.

"Is it always so quiet here?" I asked.

Zachary seemed puzzled at my comment and then realized what I was asking. "We're still getting things set up and getting known. We're now on most of the hotel sites, so people know about us, and we're getting prices arranged to make enough money, but not so much that it keeps people away. I'm sure that in a few years I'll be able to raise them slowly, but for now, it's a fine line to walk. We're not a resort, at least not yet, and we're not known, which works against us."

"It must be hard to start up a hotel." I paused to look at a large rather thorny bush. I hadn't noticed it before. It was a kind of vine, thick like a wisteria, though this one had thorns around it. I saw no flowers. I wondered if it was a very old rose bush but it was thick with green leaves that didn't seem very rose-like.

"Richard didn't think it was a good idea," Zachary said.

I looked over, puzzled, wondering who Richard was.

"Richard Perlette," Zachary clarified. "He runs the desk but he knows the estate probably better than I do because it's always been his job to know. We grew up almost together, although he's a bit older than I am, so he got to show me where things were. He was like a big brother, sometimes a rather disapproving one."

That made me smile. Richard, the desk clerk, certain did have that disapproving big brother thing going on. I wasn't even thinking about him as a brother and I thought he was disapproving, judging.

"He's very efficient," I said. "And it was quite nice of him to lead me out of here yesterday."

Zachary cleared his throat but said nothing more. We passed a genuine rose this time, although with the cloud cover and the bushes, it seemed far too shadowed in that part of the garden for roses to grow. Still, there was a single red rose on the vine. I breathed in the fragrance as we passed, marveling at how strong it was.

"Do you like roses?" Zachary asked.

"Doesn't everyone?"

He gave me the smallest of chuckles as we kept walking slowly through the gardens. Here and there he'd point out a plant that meant something to him. There was a patch of lavender that his grandmother had started but which had been divided "a thousand times," he said. It was still growing and thriving in a sun patch. Another bush, a name I wasn't familiar with, had been planted by his uncle to ward off colds. Zachary didn't credit it much and the plant wasn't as well cared for as the lavender. I wondered if Zachary himself came out to care for the lavender.

We made a turn, towards the left, going further into the garden where the trees and bushes were taller and closer together, and came face to face with a young couple. The young man was in his late teens, I thought, and the girl even younger. She was dressed in shorts and a double covering of tank top. Her feet were in red flip-flops.

"Mr. Kernroote!" the boy said.

"Cam," Zachary said carefully. "I didn't know you'd brought a friend here."

"Ye…ah," Cam replied slowly, looking from Zachary and I to the young woman. He was dark-haired, his eyes deeply shadowed, the cream of his skin standing starkly out in the shade. He reminded me of Richard, the desk clerk although he was thinner, not yet filled like he would be as a man, although in height he was only an inch shorter than Zachary, who was taller than the desk clerk if I remembered correctly. Still, I had a feeling Cam was Richard's son.

"Your friend?" Zachary asked.

"This is Trish," Cam said. "I thought it would be okay to show her the gardens?"

I couldn't figure out why he'd feel so strange about walking in the gardens. Surely they were public or at least semi-public around the hotel. It wasn't as if there were so many guests the two would intrude upon them.

"It's quite fine." Even I could tell from Zachary's tone of voice things were anything but. The smiles that the two young people wore faded and they hurried out of the garden.

I was trying to figure out why it would be a problem for them to be in the garden when Zachary spoke.

"They're nice enough kids, but the other day they were

caught in a rather indelicate situation. Richard has had come out here to hunt for them on more than one occasion. I hate to have to chase them off in front of guests, but I suspect it would ruin the hotel's reputation if one of the older couples went walking through here and found the two of them only partly dressed."

I laughed a little letting, his explanation lighten the mood. We continued walking through the garden, the dark and light areas. I started to smell the skunk smell that I had noticed yesterday but Zachary didn't comment on it as we walked. It got stronger, and we turned a corner to pass through some bushes and low trees that made the way so dark I felt as if we were approaching night. The clouds in the sky had gotten darker and I had a feeling we were in for a soaking soon enough.

Zachary turned onto a narrower path that I didn't think I had seen when I was walking the day before. Of course there were many things I hadn't noticed then because I was busy hurrying around trying to find a way out. Still, it seemed as if if I had passed such a path, I would have remembered. It was just a T sort of intersection of paths, and the one he took was so narrow that we had to turn sideways to pass between two large flowering bushes that had a fragrance that reminded me of an old lady's sachet.

"The bushes need to be trimmed," Zachary muttered as if this were news. He'd just been down here the other day, or at least Richard had.

I said nothing, following him through. This path was dark, and there were several dwarf trees that stood a little taller than I did, their branches reaching out like skeletal arms. I knew I hadn't walked this path before. All my wanderings had taken me through bushes and flowers with small trees as accents.

"I don't think I found this path yesterday," I said.

"You probably wouldn't," Zachary said. His usual charm had an edge to it. "It's hard enough to find when you know where it is. Richard shouldn't have let it get so overgrown. He'll need to talk to the gardener."

I wondered why Zachary couldn't do that but said nothing. It was cooler in this part of the garden. And silent. Our feet no longer made sounds as they crunched on the gravel, or if they did, the sounds were muted. I felt like I had cotton in my ears.

We made a curve to the left and then we were on the far side of the pond I had seen the day before. This wasn't the happy pond with the frog. This was the dead pond. And it looked even more ominous here this morning. The sky had turned nearly black with the clouds and I waited for the rain. I almost wanted the rain to fall because I needed to know that the real world would penetrate this place. It felt more dreamlike than many of my dreams had lately.

"What is this place?" I asked. It was a safe enough question. If I was hallucinating—perhaps because of the intoxicant in one of those flowers, though surely the bushes had just been camellias—it wouldn't sound strange.

"This is the exterior heart of the estate," Zachary said without looking at me. There was a reverence in his voice. "Do you see it?"

"I see a pond." I refused to elaborate on just how ugly the pond I saw was.

Zachary's head snapped to look at me. There was something in his look, almost disgust that crossed his face, but then I heard someone moving. Which was strange when I couldn't seem to hear my own feet moving the gravel around.

Zachary turned away again, towards the sound. "I wonder who that is?" His voice was once again mild and charming.

"I don't know."

He turned and gave me a smile. "Well, it seems as if the garden is unusually busy today. But I did want to show you the pond."

When I looked back the pond was lovely, with the water lily that had been near blooming yesterday in full pink bloom this morning. The frog croaked, a half croak as if in question. And the smells of water and flowers and the earth reached my nose. The black clouds floated on a bit, leaving us with dark gray clouds.

Zachary looked up. "We'll probably need to make a run for it soon. It's too bad we couldn't enjoy this longer, but I have a feeling we're going to get soaked."

"I've been noticing," I said.

We hurried off in the other direction. Shortly before we reached the entrance to the maze, we found Richard hurrying towards us.

"Ah. You must have been the one to find Cam, then," he said quickly, before Zachary could say anything.

"I did," Zachary said. His voice was ice, the tone of a man used to being the boss.

Richard gave him a nod, not smiling. "I have spoken to him. Again."

"Have you?" Zachary asked. Clearly there was disbelief, although I wasn't sure what was going on.

Rain started to fall in large drops.

"We should get inside," Zachary said to me. "And we'll continue this discussion later." He looked over at Richard.

We all hurried out of the garden, following the long, turning path to the main entrance. Richard followed behind us. If there were shadowed areas, I didn't see them, but the rain had me hurrying along, not noticing the plants. If Zachary had other stories, he wasn't sharing as we moved along.

Finally we were out of the garden, and we all ran up the stairs. Zachary kept a hand on my elbow. It was sweet and very nice of him to do that, but I was still feeling odd from our time in the garden. Had he seen the dead pond? Or was I just going crazy? I wanted to shake off the feeling but had no clue how to do so. I knew that so long as Zachary was there, it wouldn't happen.

Zachary let go of my elbow long enough to open the back door for me and I hurried in. The chill air conditioning hit my wet body and I shivered suddenly, realizing just how wet I was.

"We really got soaked," I said. I was still sort of laughing. It would be a good memory if anything came of this relationship with Zachary.

He gave me an indulgent smile, as if he were a father and I a silly child. That turned me cold.

"I'm sorry our outing ended so poorly," he replied, stiffly, formal, as though he were a lord and I was a peasant.

I was annoyed. Just because he was good looking didn't mean I'd just fall all over him, no matter how he acted.

"I'll make sure that there are more towels in Miss Winter's room," Richard said. He gave me a tight smile and a short nod before passing us in the lobby.

"I'm sorry it ended that way too," I told Zachary. "Up until that point, it was an interesting look through a very different garden."

He gave me a long look and then he smiled, as if the formality had been for Richard's sake. "I hope that perhaps you'll let me make it up to you. Perhaps dinner tomorrow night? I can't take tonight off here, but tomorrow? If that's not too forward?"

"I think I can manage that," I said.

"About six, then? I'll drive you into town. Nothing too fancy, of course. It's not that sort of town."

"Of course," I said.

Chapter 9

Upstairs, the hallway seemed longer and narrower than before, like when you're in a dream and perspective is all off. I had to put a hand to the wall—which felt like a normal wall— my disorientation was that great. I wouldn't have been surprised if the building had moved while I was walking through it, a sort of psychedelic walk, if you will.

Once inside my room, I leaned back against the door and looked over the shadowed room. Someone had already been in to clean it. I hadn't seen anyone cleaning rooms here but the place never failed to be tidied with fresh towels and the bed made. I was still dripping and I grabbed one of the towels. As I wiped my face and wrapped one around my hair, still slightly shivering, I wondered if I'd see the person delivering the extra towels Richard had promised or if more would just magically appear.

I pulled off my shorts and shirt and laid them over the tub, and changed into sweats and a T-shirt. I wasn't planning on going out again. I needed to do some writing. A knock sounded on the door, a loud thunder that made me jump. The sound would have been more appropriate for a movie giant's footsteps across the floor than it was as a knock. I hurried over to the door and opened it, not even thinking to look out the peephole.

The young man I had seen in the garden, Richard's son—Cam, if I remembered correctly—stood there looking down. He was still in jeans and a short sleeved shirt, his hair a mess.

"Your towels." He said it with a certain level of sullenness but he also managed to convey a certain level of respect. He wasn't angry with me, at least I got that.

"Thank you," I said. "I'm sorry that I came along and ruined your outing."

He looked up at me, startled that I would remember him or perhaps that I would mention that.

"My fault," he mumbled, turning to leave.

I wanted to say more, to say something like, *That's what all kids do*, but that would sound patronizing. Still, I felt as if he were being held to standards that were incredibly unfair. I let him go and closed the door, thankful for the extra towels but confident that I wouldn't need them. I settled in on the sofa to write.

An hour later, I realized I wasn't as in the flow as I had been the night before. Zachary and the meeting for the garden walk had fired me up. Unfortunately, it wasn't in a good way. I was still grumpy with his parting words, despite the offer of dinner. Now, my characters were struggling to get together but at the moment they weren't even sure they liked each other. It wasn't out of the realm of romance but the way they were going, this story could end up being anything but.

I stood up, sighing. I looked outside. The rain had

stopped for the moment but there were more clouds on the horizon. I went out on the balcony.

It was quiet outside and I frowned, feeling frustrated with the lack of noise. Didn't people go places to avoid noise? This silence was something different. It was the difference between going to a quiet restaurant to be alone and sitting in a building that had been empty for a decade.

Then I heard a car start and the tires crunch softly on the gravel. It was faint but it was there. If there had the usual amount of noise in the place, likely I wouldn't even have noticed the sounds, but here I did. I glanced down at the garden, surprised by how many shadows were moving between the plants. From here, there seemed to be several shadowy groups of people wandering around down in the maze.

I had half a mind to go down and join them if that's what was happening, but I stayed upstairs and watched. The older couple that I had seen the first morning, or at least a couple that looked much like them, exited the garden together. They were talking animatedly. Certainly they couldn't have seen the place as I had seen it, I thought.

I slipped back into my room and closed the door. It was surprisingly humid outside. No doubt it would rain again soon enough—perhaps we'd even have a thunderstorm. It hit me then that the hotel could lose power. I wondered what sort of backup systems they had. I had no desire to go down that hallway and have to use the stairs if the power was out.

I went back to the seating area and tried to call my sister. There was no answer on her phone, but I did see she'd texted me earlier. I responded that way to let her know I had gotten it. I paced around for a little bit and then tried to get back to writing.

Tried was the key word. Weird things were creeping up. For example, I had questions about whether my hero was a serial killer. I deleted the way that was going because it wasn't where I wanted my light and fluffy romance to end up. I wanted this to be slightly spicy but definitely a mainstream contemporary romance, and it kept trying to break free from those bonds and become something other. Something I didn't want to write.

I rubbed my eyes as I put the computer aside. I changed into jeans and decided to go out and do some shopping. I could get a quick bite, perhaps a late enough lunch that I would be happy with the snacks I had in the room. I could then buy a few things, like maybe a flashlight and those candles for around the tub.

That decided, I left the room. I heard someone moving quickly behind me as I made sure the door was locked. I thought I saw someone turn the far corner, quickly and furtively. Was there someone else up in the hallway? Perhaps they were working on the room that had the opened door. I felt a chill that had nothing to do with the drenching I had had earlier and walked towards the elevator, glancing behind me.

There were no special effects as I walked down the hallway this time. Perhaps there was something in the scent of the flowers in the garden. Maybe I was just allergic or something, and my reaction was to see things that weren't there rather than just sneeze like a normal person.

At the elevator I looked to the side, but the jog of the hallway meant I couldn't see anything down that way. I sighed. The doors opened, startling me. I realized that the hotel didn't even have a bell for when the elevator reached the floor, which seemed strange. Didn't that always happen? Maybe this hadn't been turned on yet because they were still expanding.

I rode down to the lobby in silence, alone.

No one was at the desk. It wasn't raining when I went out to my car. There was a different young man in uniform today. I wondered if this young man only worked the weekends. He was kicking dirt and clearly had earbuds in. Still he gave me a smile and a wave as I left the hotel. I waved back, thankful that at least someone here seemed friendly in a normal sort of way.

I drove out of the parking area and down the long, narrow drive. I passed no other cars coming in, but there was a fair amount of traffic on the road by the mansion, so I had to wait at the gates while listening to an advertisement for a spa treatment at a ritzy place in Asheville. As the announcer was giving the phone and website, I was able to make the right-hand turn and head towards the highway.

It was cloudy enough that I didn't need sunglasses, which was nice. The roads were only slightly damp so they shouldn't have been too slippery, and there were no accidents. I breathed in the fresh mountain air, realizing even in the outdoors around the mansion the air felt canned, as if I were housed inside a giant auditorium or something.

I filed that away. The castle was clearly a strange place. Really I ought to be writing a horror novel, except I'd probably have to leave and stay somewhere else.

I saw a few signs for big box stores and pulled off. I wandered around one of the big hardware stores for a while, looking at things I had no need of, but enjoying the sounds of people talking, the echoing voices in the high-ceilinged room, the sounds of beeping machinery as it backed up, and the conversations of normal human people. I found a set of flashlights and I purchased those.

When I left, I noticed that the clouds were lower but still not terribly dark. I drove down the road a little further and found a dollar store. I pulled in there to look for a cheap lighter, which I had forgotten. I'd also see what kind of candles they had.

I found the lighter easily enough, having to push past a large young man who wasn't paying attention to anything. He didn't say "Excuse me," but he lumbered off when I got to the lighters, clearly bored with shopping. It was rude, but it was a more normal rudeness. I was nearly run down by a lady with a cart that held an assortment of odds and ends, everything from glasses to a pan to several towels. Setting up home from the dollar store.

I found a few candles. One had a horrible scent and reminded me of the skunk scent that I'd smelled in the garden overlaid with lavender. There were unscented votive candles in yellow, but they were a pleasant yellow, and I got a package of four of those. I would need something to sit them on, just in case so I looked around and found cheap small votive holders, just a glass holder that vaguely looked like a rose.

Good enough. I got four of those so I could light all four candles around the tub later on. And I had the flashlight if the power went out. I maneuvered my way through the people, passing by two girls wearing jeans that were cut so low a line of skin along their butts were showing, avidly looking at makeup. They didn't even notice as I brushed by them in the crowded aisles that had extra displays of special items in between them.

I had to wait next to the candy stand where they were selling chocolate and peanut butter candies. I grabbed two of those. They'd be good treats in the evening or perhaps in the afternoons as I wrote. I could promise myself one if I wrote a certain number of words that satisfied me.

When I was done, I drove around looking for a place to eat. I found a sit-down family place and went in. They were fast with their service, while once again I soaked in the noises of dishes and conversation. I smelled the spicy sauces and watched people laughing and talking. It all made me smile.

The gray-eyed man from Kernroote Castle wandered in as I was waiting. He gave me a smile and a wave. I gave him a small wave back, wondering if I should invite him over. He appeared to be alone as well. It occurred to me to wonder what he was doing there by himself. Before I could gesture to him to join me, the hostess led him to another part of the restaurant.

When I had finished eating, I noticed I was making excuses not to leave. I looked at my phone and drank the last of the soda I had ordered. I considered asking for another but was afraid the server would give me one in a to-go cup as a hint. I didn't want to return to Kernroote, but I had no idea why not.

I used up all my mental excuses and finally had to get back in the car and return. There was no reason for me to dislike the place so much. But, in fact, it occurred to me that I did hate it. I hated the silence of it. I hated the lack of scent. I hated that there were too few people in too large of a space. I wanted a normal, orderly hotel. Unfortunately, I had booked a special price, which meant I would lose the money I had spent on my vacation if I left early.

I sighed. I had enough, but not so much that I could afford to just toss that kind of cash out the window. I could afford to drive home to Charlotte, although I had rented my condo, not sold it, so I'd have to kick someone out and do my writing there, but I suspected that the familiarity of home would keep me from writing every bit as much as the unfamiliarity of the castle. Perhaps I was just impossible to please.

At least I'd had a normal meal. It started to rain about

the time I reached the black iron gates of Kernroote. The rain slowed forced me to drive even slower than normal along the entrance road. The graveled drive wasn't as smooth as I had thought and there were pools of water in some places, even now. I hadn't thought that it was raining for that long or even that hard. I was glad to make the turn and see the place waiting for me.

There was a depressing air about it when there wasn't any sun. Nothing gleamed as it had in the sunshine and the areas that needed repair seemed highlighted in the poor light and the rain. I thought I saw a window cracked up on the sixth floor but couldn't be sure. A trick, certainly, otherwise there would be damage not only to that room but to the room below.

I parked in the lot and gathered my things. I sat in the car, listening to the radio and the patter of the raindrops until the little storm passed far enough that I could run to the portico. There were more cars here today than there had been, but the place would still hold empty rooms even if every single one of us were on the same floor.

I wondered about asking if I could be moved to a lower floor. I was unpacked and hated to have to move all my stuff. I'd think about it a little more.

The things I put up with out of sheer laziness, I thought. An older couple was going up the stairs to the second floor. They were both in shorts and shirts and had hair that looked like pale white cotton candy. They moved easily, though, up the wide wooden stairs, but they were quiet, not speaking. Perhaps they had spoken to each other in the lobby but the sounds had sounded too loud, so now they were just walking, exploring, or perhaps hoping for an early dinner.

I made my way over the elevator. I glanced at the desk. I thought I saw Richard move in the background but if he had, he was only a shadow, like so many things around the mansion. I had no wait for the elevator, which I rode up the fifth floor. I considered going up the sixth floor to explore there, but perhaps that would be better done when it wasn't late in the afternoon on a stormy evening.

I made my way down the hallway, avoiding the shadows that always seemed to be longer than the day before. Soon enough it would be full dark and the lights would still be on, I thought. No doubt all of that was just my imagination.

I got to my room and set my things down after closing the door. The air was still on, blowing cool air into the room. The clouds outside were making the place seem darker than it normally did. I turned on all the lights once again, but didn't like the way the shadows moved. In fact, they moved most nearest the window, probably as birds flew or something.

I could watch television in the chair, but it would require turning my back on the bed area and those shadows. Ironically, it seemed safer to be part of their dance and keep an eye on them than it did to stay in the other room with my back turned.

I climbed into the bed and flipped channels until I found a 1980s comedy movie to watch. I settled in to enjoy the laughter. I tried to relax. I was enjoying the comfort of the bedsheets when the television brightened and then popped and went dead.

The lights were still on in the room but there was a sound coming from above, like a groan. I pushed myself off the bed and looked up. Then there was a thump. I was halfway to the phone on the desk before I realized that this could be like the knocking on the door and just an echo. Perhaps I didn't want to move to a lower room if things from upstairs sounded like this.

I was calming my beating heart, despite the continued noise, when someone pounded on my door. I jumped and hurried over there, wondering who would be there. Perhaps Zachary had come back to apologize for this morning. Or perhaps there was something wrong.

I used the peephole this time but there was no one out there. I opened the door and looked out. I thought I saw a shadow turn the corner to other wing but that was all.

I closed the door and leaned back against it. The booming knock came again. I leaped, turning, stepping back, trying to decide if I should open the door again or if I should put a chair in front of it.

Chapter 10

I backed up a little, listening. Had I just been complaining that it was too quiet? I went for the desk and called down there.

"Front desk." It sounded like Richard's bored voice.

"I think something just happened with the television set in my room," I said. "And there's some sort of pounding upstairs?"

"When it storms sometimes the water does that upstairs. I will have someone come up and check on the television now. If it's not fixable, we can move you to another room if you'd like."

"Yes, if you can't fix it, I think I'd like that. Perhaps to a room that's not on the fifth floor," I said.

"I'll have to check and see what we have available. Your package included an upgrade to the balcony room and not all our rooms have balconies." There was concern in the voice for not meeting my expectations.

"I understand," I said.

I put the phone down and walked back to the door, which was now quiet. Was there any way that the pounding been an echo from the top floor? I looked out through the peephole but there was no one waited. I sighed.

This was getting ridiculous. If the television didn't work I should demand to be put down on the first or second floor. At least that way if the lights did go out, I could make my way downstairs more easily. Oddly, I had no desire to climb down the main winding stair from this floor, although I couldn't have said why.

A few minutes later there was another pounding on the door. I was still standing there, thinking about what I wanted to do. Still I hesitated looking out the peep hole, but forced myself to do so. It was Cam, this time dressed in a uniform of black and white, similar to what his father wore but a little more utilitarian.

I opened it.

"You had a problem with the television?" he asked.

I nodded. "It's the one in front of the bed."

"The big one?" He seemed surprised. "Those are nice sets. Dad got an awesome deal for Mr. Kernroote."

I noticed the way he referred to Zachary. I wondered if he always talked about him like that or if he was just conscious he was with a guest. But it sounded very polite.

Cam moved easily over to the television. He felt around behind it and checked the plugs. "This is such an old hotel that sometimes the outlets get funky and things just kind of fall out or act like they'll short out, but the plugs come out of the outlet. No one ever gets it when I explain what I think is going on. I guess newer homes don't have that happen."

"Do you live here, then?" I asked. It surprised me to think that Richard might live on site. Zachary, I could see. He had inherited the place, but the way he'd said that Richard's family had always worked there and he'd essentially inherited them, that sort of living arrangement made sense.

"Yeah," Cam said. "We're up on the seventh floor. Great views but if we get that thunderstorm tonight…" He grunted something as he worked with the television and the plug. "Well, thunderstorms make a lot of noise. You'll probably get some of that even here. Dad said you heard something upstairs?"

I nodded. Whatever was up there thumped helpfully and then the racket began again.

"Water. In the pipes," Cam said. "Don't know why the storms do that. It's like the whole place is an old woman getting all crotchety when the weather isn't nice."

I smiled to hear such a young person use the words he did, but it seemed like an apt description of the old building. My fears were clearly my imagination running wild. I was pretty certain that was it when Cam picked up the remote and turned on the television and it started.

"Course, the fifth floor is better in some ways. At least you don't have the noises from the restaurant echoing down to your room like on the first and second floors. Dad told Mr. Kernroote we should do the rooms on the lower levels of the wings before the upstairs but Mr. Kernroote had his reasons for choosing to renovate the way he did, I guess."

"Thank you so much for fixing this," I said. I really was grateful. I tipped him this time, as I'd called. Before, the extra towels had been the idea of the desk clerk. I probably should have given him something but I hadn't quite been myself.

Cam left and I turned to look around the room. There were still shadows. I sighed. The thumping came from the ceiling again, like giants dancing and then faded away. Something pounded on the door again. I looked out, in case Cam had returned but there was no one there. Was this going to go on all night?

I could call back down to the desk and demand that I get a different room because this one was so noisy, I supposed. But it sounded as if the first and second floors had their own echoes. The advantage there would be that I knew those were people making those noises. Of course, who knew?

I settled back on the bed and tried to watch television. It was light and funny but the noises kept me from really settling, although I did get a bit used to them. When the rain started to fall, I hardly noticed. As it got darker, I saw a few flashes of lightening and then heard the long rolls of thunder. The water pipes upstairs paused, as if listening to real thunder and taking notes on how to do it right.

I smiled at my fancy. Too bad I wasn't trying to write a horror novel or even what they called dark fantasy. This was clearly the perfect place for such a writing retreat. No, I was trying to write romance, which wasn't coming along at all.

My phone rang, startling me in its ordinariness.

"Hey Kara," I said, after looking at the number and realizing it was my sister.

"I saw you called. How is the castle?"

"Noisy." At that moment the thumping began again upstairs. The curtains moved but I felt the slightest chill breeze so it must have been the air conditioning. I turned down the television as Kara and I began to chat. I told her about my walk with Zachary, leaving out the weird parts of the pond. I tried to figure out how I could ask her about the scents and perhaps hallucinogenic flowers.

She chatted about her last few shifts, which were, as always, busy. She liked urgent care and ER nursing because she hated being bored. I listened and let her voice and her normal days wash over me.

She talked about a patient using drugs who thought they saw a monster coming out of the bathroom and they were sure the monster hadn't washed its hands. Like being eaten by a monster who hadn't washed after flushing was worse than being eaten by a monster who had.

But it gave me the perfect opening to ask about flowers.

"I can't think of anything offhand," Kara said. "But if you're having symptoms, send me some images. And likely, you'd feel strange more than just start seeing things."

"Good to know," I said. "I just felt strange there and I thought I saw something out of the corner of my eye and, well, the monster in the bathroom reminded me of it." None of that was a lie, but it was certainly leaving a huge amount of strange stuff out. I didn't want Kara getting all freaked out and rushing out to make sure I was okay.

Thunder rolled in and clapped loud enough that Kara gave a small scream and then asked, "What was that?"

"Thunder," I said. "You should hear the pipes upstairs. I guess when it rains it sounds like dinosaurs and giants are running around up there."

"Can they change your room?" Kara asked. "That's horrible. And I mean not just the thunder but that their plumbing is so noisy."

"The television went out earlier and the young man who came up to fix it said it gets pretty noisy down on the first and second floors. I suppose I could ask to be on the third floor but who knows. There are weird acoustics here."

"Yeah. I might be sorry I recommended it," Kara said. "Are you sleeping okay?"

Sleep was the one thing I was doing quite well at, I thought. "That's great. They have the best beds. I guess the way they've been remodeling them, I might be the first person to get to sleep on this one. Can you imagine?"

"Well, that's something. I just don't know about this place, though. I suppose the rate I got you wasn't refundable if you wanted to go somewhere else?" Kara asked.

"I'm pretty sure it's not. I was planning on looking into that if tonight is horrible. If I can't sleep, then maybe I'll ask to be moved downstairs or something."

Kara acknowledged the wisdom of such a plan and then rang off. I settled in to watch television. Just as I was relaxing, despite the noise that still kind of freaked me out, the television and the lights went out.

I was left in the dark. When nothing flickered on, I swore softly at myself. I had left the bags with the candles and the flashlights across the room. I patted the covers, but couldn't find my cell phone. It was darker in there than I'd expected. There were no lights outside. I'd never been in such a dark hotel.

I felt my way around the bed, always hoping to find my cell phone and perhaps use it to light the way to my purchases. Nothing. Still, I made it around to the low wall. I held my hands out to where I thought I'd left the bag. I felt around in it, thankful that I'd found it so easily. I found the batteries I'd purchased first and I sat down on the floor.

My fingers felt around the flashlight package. I managed to rip off the heavy cardboard it was attached to.

Noise thundered above me, making my hands shake a little as I did so.

I couldn't remember how the flashlight had looked, but I felt around until I found the bottom of it and tried to screw it off like a cap.

Something pounded on my door so hard I imagined the thing falling inward, with me sitting there with nothing but a half-assembled flashlight, in the dark. My imagination built up a monster creeping towards me. Though my hands shook, I managed to unscrew the bottom cap.

I dropped the battery I was holding, even as I waited to feel a cool hand on my shoulder or my hands. Or maybe a claw.

My fingers searched for the dropped battery. I couldn't see anything in the pitch blackness. Finally I grabbed on to something and carefully tried to drop it into the tube that was the open flashlight, working only by feel.

I reached for the battery package for a second one when the thundering pounding came again. I think I squeaked in fear, like a little mouse. My imagination was getting the better of me.

I worked harder to grab one of the batteries and put that into the flashlight and screwed the cap back on. I turned it on, hoping I had guessed right as to which direction they needed to go.

I breathed a sigh when the light came on.

I flashed the light around the room. I started when I saw a long, dark shadow that looked like a tree branch reaching across the room. My breathing quickened but the look faded and it was just another long shadow from the ceiling.

My heart pounded as I looked through the bags for the candles. I placed those out on the coffee table.

I lighted my way to the phone and dialed the front desk. I got a message saying they were experiencing higher than normal volume and they would get back to me as soon as they could if I'd just leave a message. I hung up.

How many guests did they have? I wondered. Other than the thumps and thunder, I hadn't heard anything that sounded particularly human and normal out in the hallway. No television, not even a human scream as the lights went out. It wasn't that late so others must have been surprised by the power failure.

I could go down the stairs but I didn't even want to think of that. The thundering pounding came on my door. I looked out but it was just black. I was backing up but a bright eye-shaped thing shone in the room. I backed up with a start.

The knob of my door turned back and forth as if someone was trying to get in. I had the locks set and I made sure to put on the small latch that wouldn't be likely to keep out a determined intruder, but it made me feel better.

I waited. Nothing happened. I looked out again. It was dark.

I sighed. I didn't like this. I was definitely moving rooms the next day. I went back to the front desk and tried to call.

"Front desk," came the answer. It sounded like Richard but he was almost breathless, less disapproving in his tone.

"I'm just wondering if there was an estimate on when the power might be back on," I said.

"The power is on," he said, puzzled. "I'll go check the fuses and see if there's something going on on the fifth floor. Let me get back to you."

"Thank you. And perhaps if there is a problem we can discuss having my room changed," I said.

"Of course." He hung up before I could say anything else.

What a jerk. And great. Only this floor or even just this part of a floor was in the dark. I wondered how long it would take if the fuses were out. I wanted to pace, but it was too dark to do that. Now and then shadows would trail across the room like waving branches reaching out towards me, which sent chills down my back.

The air conditioning had clearly gone off up here and sweat trailed down my back now, which meant that when I saw the shadows I was hot and cold at the same time. It was as if my outer body were on fire, but deep down I was chilled. My heart was beating way too fast and my hands were sweating. I was clutching the one flashlight like I thought if I let go, I'd die. The other was on the table in the seating area.

I glanced over there and thought I saw a white shape move low to the carpet. Where there rats in the hotel?

My toes curled in alarm and I stood on one foot, holding the other up to my leg. I leaned around, trying to get a glimpse of what that might have been. I took a tentative step forward, shining the flashlight on the floor. Nothing there. And there was nothing that I could see in the other part of the room.

I took another slow step, shining the light down on the floor and then around while I tentatively put my foot down. I walked four steps this way and I was in the other room, toes curled to make sure my feet were as small of a target as possible, but I saw nothing scurrying around in there. In fact, not even a shadow moved.

My heart was still pounding wildly at the thought of this new threat, a threat that I could see and understand, unlike the shadows and hallucinations, when the phone rang, making me jump nearly out of my skin.

"Hello?" I said.

There was no sound on the other end.

"Hello?" I said louder.

There was a bit of static.

"Hello?"

Nothing. I put the phone down, frustrated, and considered calling the front desk again when the pounding came on the door.

I hurried over to the door to look out, expecting to see nothing, worried I'd see that blinding flash of light but as I got there, the lights in my room came on. I looked out. Nothing was there. I turned, but my room looked normal again.

This time when the phone rang, it was Richard at the front desk calling to be sure that my room was fine.

"Very good," he said, hanging up before I could broach the subject of changing rooms again.

The television was on but it was no comfort now. In fact, during the time the lights were off, it had switched from a comedy to one of those hack-and-slash horror flicks. I changed the channel until I found another light movie with soothing music and a loud laugh track. I left it on, along with all the lights, while I went to the bathroom.

I saw no rats or even so much as a fly while I looked around. I did find my phone, on floor beneath the edge of the bed. I was lucky I hadn't stepped on it.

After huddling on the bed watching the television, I decided I needed to do something relaxing and normal. I'd take a bath.

I took my clothing off and ran the water as hot as I could stand it. It was clear and fresh and I spent some time lighting candles to put in the corners where the shadows seemed to hide. All in all, this might be just what I needed.

What I really needed, I thought, lowering myself into the tub, still listening to the laugh track, was some good music, but I was loath to turn off the television. I didn't want to move. The hot bath was soothing and I leaned back and listened to the laughter, fantasizing that I was in a room filled with people and we were all talking and laughing.

I thought I heard someone walk down the hall as I sat there, hurried feet as if they couldn't wait to get to their room. To further my suspicion, there was the tiniest creak of a door and the faintest click of closing. I hoped whoever they were, they were just across the way, so that I could hear them now and again and not feel so alone, particularly if the thundering from upstairs came again.

It was mercifully quiet for the moment and I intended to use that time to relax. I would have liked to say that I nearly fell asleep, but my thoughts continued to race around in circles, trying to make sense of Kernroote Castle. When I tried to switch to more pleasant thoughts about Zachary, I was reminded of the garden and my hallucination. There was something wrong with this place, but I had no idea what it was.

If I were a character in my romance, Zachary would be there trying to help me figure it out. Chances were Richard would be the one creating the illusion that I was hallucinating so he wouldn't lose his master. Or perhaps he'd have a sister that he wanted Zachary to marry or some such thing. Or maybe Zachary had let Richard's wife die by accident and now Richard didn't want to see Zachary happy ever again. Whatever that was, I had a villain.

If I were in a mystery, I'd be required to go out and start investigating. If I were in a bad mystery, I'd do it tonight. In a decent one, I'd get a good night's sleep, make notes about what I wanted to find out, and do it in the morning. Perhaps there rooms that were only half finished offered clues and I'd start there.

The horror novel of all of this didn't bear thinking about, at least not until I was safely away, and even then I'd need to be careful, just in case thinking about the name of the castle brought the evils back to me.

The water cooled and I stepped out to dry off and then perhaps climb into bed. Once again, I had no plans to turn off the lights. I even considered leaving the television on, but when I crawled under the covers, the shadows on the ceiling that came from the show that was playing bothered me so I turned it off.

I tried to sleep. Somewhere in the middle of the night, the banging from upstairs came again. I startled from my half doze and then realized what it was. Someone banged on the door to my room, or rather it sounded like someone banging on the door. I was starting to think that might have been the way the sound traveled. Perhaps it was something upstairs that made it sound like someone knocking.

I pulled the covers up closer and dozed back off, although I didn't sleep as soundly as I had the other nights. I was definitely going to ask for a room change in the morning.

Chapter 11

I woke the next morning but I wasn't refreshed at all. I was grumpy and tired. I felt as if I were getting a headache from lack of sleep. I looked outside and it was sunny again. In fact, things had quieted down in the wee hours of the morning, so I suspected that the weather system had moved through about that time. Not that it helped me sleep at all. I woke several times from strange dreams of running through a cave.

It was earlier than I wanted, but I couldn't get back to sleep even though I finally turned off some, but not all, the lights in the room. I dressed in another pair of capris and a casual top. I'd consider what to wear for dinner later. I was locking my room, getting ready to go down to breakfast, when I saw someone come out of a room towards the end of the hallway. They didn't turn towards me. Instead they went down the unfinished wing, probably to the stairwell.

I followed, thinking perhaps that they knew what they were doing. The door at the far end of the wing was just closing when I got to where the corridor turned the corner. I was surprised at how fast the person had walked. The long corridor was more than twice as far as the distance from my room to where I now stood.

I walked more slowly down this hallway. The lights were working today. None of them were flickering more than the normal amount for fluorescent bulbs. They did buzz, but that was almost a normal sound. Several doors were partly open today. I hadn't heard anyone working but someone must have been. I pushed one of them open a little further. The smell of dead skunk wafted out and I backed up.

The room, what I could see of it, was like the other one. Mostly carpeted but with a plastic cover over it. The walls were down to the drywall as far as I could tell and the area that would be the bathroom was only framed in.

I walked on. I heard the sound of something falling behind me. I turned but I saw no one. I considered going back to the room to look in but decided that would be foolish. I hurried along, noting the doors that were ajar, looking in, but not too closely, and heading for the stairwell. Once there, I opened the door, an industrial steel door of gray that blended with the wall surprisingly well. There was a small window in the door. It was heavier than I expected when I opened it and headed down.

The fourth floor was dark, as if there weren't even lights in that wing, and I hurried by, not wanting a repeat of the performance where the lighted eyes of something looked at me through a peephole. This window was far too big and my imagination conjured far too many monsters for me to be comfortable standing anywhere near it.

The third floor was lit but the bulbs flickered and there was a buzz that could be heard even in the stairwell. I didn't like it, but at least there was noise and not the absurd silence that enveloped the rest of the place.

The second floor looked as normal as any place and I

wondered if that wing had been finished. I decided to walk down that hall, seeing it looked so inviting, but the door was stuck. I pushed several times but the handle didn't even turn. Apparently it was locked.

I went down to the first floor, suddenly nervous that I would be locked in the stairwell. Once there, I pushed against the door and once again, nothing. I tried to turn the knob but there was nothing. I looked around for an outside door. A stairwell should work as a fire escape. Half a set of stairs down, I saw another door. I went to that and it opened, only it didn't open to the outside, but to another set of stairs with another door at the bottom.

It was darker down that set of stairs and I considered whether I wanted to go down those or run up to the fifth floor and have a try at the exit there. I decided head down to the lower door. This was a hotel and while my imagination was running wild, I hadn't seen any ghosts. Even if I did, I didn't think ghosts, real ghosts, could actually hurt anyone. But what did I know?

I got to bottom of the steps, noticing that this was an older door, made of wood. The knob was brass and worn but it turned easily. Opening it to dim light, I saw that I was indeed in a hallway in what would be the basement. Pipes were overhead against a low ceiling. I heard the typical knocking of hot water pipes echoing around down there. It was almost comforting.

There were lights along the ceiling, plain, ordinary lights beneath ugly round plastic fixtures that had turned slightly yellow. There was a dead fly in one, which created a strange shadow that creeped me out. Still, at least there was a reason for that shadow. If anything, I felt easier in the basement than I had up in my room. Perhaps the creepiness didn't extend that deep.

I walked down the corridor. There were walls but they

weren't solid. In some places there would be a piece missing from the upper part. In another there would be an entire sheet missing, not like a doorway—it was far too wide—but as if someone hadn't bothered to finish walling in whatever was beyond the corridor. It all looked like furnace stuff and plumbing. In one corner was a new metal boxy thing that could have been a generator, but it was larger than any such generator I had ever seen.

I kept walking. My shoes echoed on the bare cement. I was surprised at the cement. I thought there was a lower level than this, and it seemed as though cement would be too heavy to be held up by beams and such. But I wasn't in construction, so I could easily be wrong.

It was cool but not too cold down here. I felt a few breaths of air that had to come from vents in the ceiling although I didn't hear an air conditioner. That surprised me, considering that I was right there and should have heard something.

I turned a corner, probably where I was under the main part of the building, and the cement became a pale cream tile. Perhaps the lower level was only under the main building. I walked on down the corridor. This area was more finished, with industrial white paneling and doors that were carefully labeled.

Steam came out of one room and I saw a door labeled Laundry. Clearly there were people around doing the laundry. Someone yelled somewhere in the basement but I couldn't quite make out the direction it had come from. Soon enough I was in front of the elevators that I normally used in the morning. I pressed the Up button.

I had to wait a few seconds for the car to come but eventually it did, the doors sliding open with their usual silent efficiency. I got in and turned around, noticing as I did so there was a room beyond the corridor that suggested that the basement continued under the parking lot. It could be a narrow room, I thought, and only ran under the garden in front. Still, it seemed like a strange layout.

But again, this was an old building, so who knew what the original footprint was like? If it had been a friendlier place, I might have considered looking at old plans and figuring out where things were.

Even in the atmosphere of the hotel as it was, if I were an investigator, I'd go out and investigate. Given the night I'd had, I had no desire to do anything of the sort and was momentarily thankful that I'd never taken up any sort of investigative position.

I rode up to the lobby and got out. I went to the desk and waited a moment, hoping to talk to Richard. But, as always, he wasn't around. There was no bell to ring and though I waited for several minutes, I didn't even see a hint of movement from anywhere around the desk. I gave up for the moment and went in to breakfast.

The sun was bright and the breakfast room looked inviting. I found a table near the window and settled in. There were at least five other tables occupied. One was occupied by a family with two children. The other tables were all couples but for a single table with the gray-eyed man who ate alone. I drew in a breath, enjoying the fact that there were people around. I wondered how their night had gone. At least one of the children looked as cranky as I felt.

The waitress, the same girl from the first day, came by to take my order. It was a breakfast quiche or pancakes with either the blueberry or peach compote. I went with the quiche. I didn't feel festive enough for pancakes.

The family started moving around as if they were leaving as I sat sipping my water. The woman picked up a large white bag. The man made sure he had his wallet.

They were probably my age. We could have been friends. Their boy was six or perhaps seven, I thought. The little girl was younger with dark curls around her head.

"Mommy," the little boy said as he passed me.

"What?" Mom was absently fiddling with her phone.

"Why does that lady have a ghost tree at her table?" The boy pointed directly at me. I saw nothing at my table.

The woman turned, a frown between her eyebrows, and she scanned the area and sighed. "What is up with you and these ghost trees?" She shook her head and ignored him.

I continued to sip my water until the waitress came back with coffee, which I drank more quickly than I probably should have. Fortunately she was there to refill it just as quickly. The caffeine kept me feeling more myself. Between the poor sleep and the boy's comment, I was starting to look around to see if I saw a ghost tree, whatever that was.

I had my quiche, which was good but not what I was craving, and then left to go back to write. I wondered how Zachary would contact me if things changed for the evening. Standing up, I brushed off a stray leaf that had apparently blown in through the air conditioner from my pants.

Chapter 12

After leaving the breakfast area, I'd waited to see if I could find Richard to talk about a change in rooms, but he wasn't around.

The gray-eyed man, who introduced himself as Chris, paused to talk to me while I waited to see if Richard would show up.

"The place is pretty nice for the cost, don't you think?" he said after he'd finally given me his name.

"Nice, yes, but a little too quiet for me," I said. "I'm hoping to move down to a lower floor. The fifth seems almost too quiet."

"I didn't realize they'd even renovated that far," Chris said. "I'd heard only the first three floors were being used. I must have read old news."

"My room does look pretty new," I said. "And there is clearly some renovation going on in the wings up there, still."

Chris nodded, awkward now that there was a pause. "I'm just hanging out here for a few days, going hiking and stuff," he said. "Maybe you'd like to join me sometime?"

"Maybe," I said, not sure how to answer. He wasn't darkly handsome like Zachary, but I felt as if I might be choosing a brooding Heathcliff over a nice man my own age with more normal interests. Really, what did I have in common with a man who inherited a place like Kernroote Castle?

Chris smiled, sort of shy, nodding and heading back towards the elevator. Part of me wanted to run after him, to chase him down, tap him on the shoulder and talk some more. Another part of me wanted to stubborn out waiting on Richard.

In the end, neither happened. Chris went back to his room alone. Perhaps five minutes later, I gave up on Richard, returning to mine.

When I'd given up, I thought I'd phone down later but the phone in my room seemed to not work when I'd tried. It was something I would mention to Zachary that evening.

Later on, after trying to write and finding it difficult, I got ready to change, taking a short shower to freshen up. I pondered how to bring up the subject of the desk clerk as I dressed carefully in a nice pair of pants—jeans, really, but chocolate colored. I added a button-down blouse in black and brown that brought out the colors in my hair and eyes. To make things a bit more festive, I put on dangling earrings and a necklace that picked up the blue in the jeans against the black and brown of the shirt.

I headed downstairs. Even then, Richard wasn't at the desk.

I found a chair in which to relax in while I waited. I was prompt but not early and the fact that Zachary was once again late didn't make me like him any better. But when he finally rushed around the corner from the elevators, looking freshly showered and shaved, a well-tailored shirt and slacks on, looking hopeful, it was hard not to be charmed. Everyone had their faults.

While I clearly quite liked the man, I wasn't thinking I'd just go out and hope that we'd be partners forever. No. I wanted to see what he was like when he wasn't at the hotel. He seemed so changeable in the castle. Was he like that everywhere or only when he was at work? Because even though we had wandered through a garden as if we were on a date, he was still the owner of the place we were touring and I was a guest. Now we would be more equal.

At least that's what I told myself.

"Becca," Zachary said when he met my eyes.

"Zachary." I waited for him to come to me. He was dressed a bit more nicely than I was, but we could definitely go to the same restaurant without embarrassment. And my shirt, with the necklace and earrings, really did dress up my outfit even if I was a little on the casual side compared to him. I had considered a sundress, but didn't want to look as if I were trying too hard. Dresses are not my forte.

"That's a lovely outfit on you."

"Thank you," I said. "You look very dressed up. I was thinking perhaps I'd made a mistake not wearing a dress."

Zachary shook his head. "It's a problem of being a hotel owner. I'm always a bit dressed up. Shall we go?" He held out his arm, a sort of old-fashioned gesture but it was a nice one. I took it. He led me back towards the main doors but instead of going out through them, he led me down the hallway by the elevators.

"Where are we going?" I asked as we passed the narrow windows with the urns of fake flowers. Then the hall turned inward after a few feet and we were passing by rooms, or so I thought.

"I have a garage out this way. It was added long after the castle was built, a sort of carriage house," he said.

"I think I've heard or read that the two wings that surround the courtyard out back are more recent additions than the front of the building," I said.

Zachary nodded. "Originally, I'm told it was just the area around the lobby, not even the full building. And it was only four stories plus the basement."

"I thought there were two lower levels on the elevator," I said.

"Don't laugh, but the land was lower then. The first basement was once part of the main floor. This place is *that* old." He looked over to me with a smile and raised eyebrows. I wasn't sure how much of the story was true because I hadn't thought people built things like this that long ago, but I said nothing more.

"And you called the garden the heart of the place," I laughed.

He sobered immediately at the mention of the garden. "The garden is the heart, and once there was a grotto there, or so I've heard. The Perlettes have always been the history keepers of the place and I trust what Richard says when he says that there was something there."

I smiled and nodded, wondering about trusting Richard with his disapproving face and eyes. *Did he disapprove of everything?* I wondered, but didn't ask. It sounded as if Richard and Zachary were old friends bound by ties that were nearly family.

We came to a doorway labeled Employees Only and Zachary opened it. Instead of going outside, we were in a large garage that housed two cars. One was an SUV in black and the other was a sporty little car, also in black. I wasn't sure what it was, but it certainly looked like fun.

"My contribution to the environment," Zachary said. "My Tesla."

"Really?" I asked.

He nodded. "I keep the SUV for longer trips, but we can more than get to the restaurant in the Tesla. It's a fun car to drive."

Like everything else about the place, the Tesla was silent. It did, however, handle well and there was a radio, not to mention the fact that Zachary actually talked.

"I hated living way out here in the boonies when I was growing up," he said. "Where did you grow up?"

"I was an army brat, really, so I've lived all over. My sister loves it but I tried putting down roots in Charlotte. It seemed like a good place with plenty of potential employers," I said. It was all safe enough stuff. No exact information and he didn't even have my sister's name. Fortunately I had a common enough last name so I didn't need to worry that he'd go all stalker on me.

"I've always lived here. Except when I went off to college," Zachary said. "I went to Ohio State. A good school but not a real interesting place. In hindsight, I should have gone further, although I did do an exchange semester in England."

"I would have loved to do that," I said, "but there's not much use for it as a business major."

Zachary nodded. "I majored in business and minored in history. I liked history and it seemed to fit the theme of the house. I had no idea what I'd do so business seemed a likely degree and would get me into anything."

"You had the inheritance didn't you?"

"Nothing is certain, of course," Zachary said. "My father impressed that on me. My mother just accepted that I would inherit, telling me never to worry. In fact, she did that the day she died, making me promise I wouldn't let worry eat at me."

"I'm sorry to hear it." I wanted to ask more but bit my tongue so I wouldn't inadvertently be offensive.

"My father lasted longer. I'm not sure that was a good thing. He died two years ago. As soon as I inherited, I started thinking about the hotel. Richard wasn't all that excited about it but you'd be shocked at how much an old place like Kernroote can cost to keep up. I'm not sure what they were thinking with the newer wings and the extra floors."

"It seemed like someone in your family must have been popular." It was an interesting thing. Who had decided that a castle like that was appropriate out in the middle of nowhere?

"I like the story that says my great-grandfather was jealous of the Biltmore so he added ostentation to the castle around that time. The timing is right, although I'm not at all certain about the motivation."

Zachary made a quick turn onto a street that seemed to go nowhere but no doubt it would bring us the back way towards a town where there was a restaurant.

"I don't know anything about my family," I said. "I think if anything makes me jealous, it's that you know your ancestry."

"It's not all good," Zachary said. "I mean I know my ancestors owned slaves, for instance, and from what I've read in the old journals and can infer, they weren't the nicest of owners. As his family was our 'white overseer,' Richard has stories, but he's kind enough not to tell them."

"I'm surprised that there is still a stipulation that his family works for yours," I said, remembering what Zachary had told me the other day.

"It's archaic, I know. But it's always been that way and

Richard won't be the one to change things. I've tried talking to Cam, but he seems bound to the household as well, although my changing the place means his duties will be different. I'm sure he'll expect to be in the will just like all his family. I can't imagine living like that."

"Neither can I," I responded. Cam seemed like a nice, level-headed young man. I wondered why he'd act like he would be tethered to such a place. He'd have so many more opportunities if he weren't tied down there. Asheville was a nice city, but I couldn't imagine not being able to go where I wanted. What if Cam loved computers and he wanted to be closer to Raleigh?

Of course, I thought, Zachary had gone off to school. Cam could do that as well. Perhaps going off to college would make him rethink his desire to be so close to Kernroote. But then again, you never knew. I didn't know why it bothered me so much to know Cam was tied to the place, except that I disliked the castle and I liked him.

The Tesla made another quick turn onto a quieter street. But I began to get a sense that we were close to a town. There were more cars passing us. Soon enough the trees and periodic houses gave way to a downtown area. I wasn't sure which town. It was too small and the wrong direction to be Asheville. Zachary pulled up outside an old log cabin sort of place.

"My friend Brian's place," he said, getting out of the car. I followed him, looking over the place. It was set on a corner, although I couldn't tell how busy the other street was. We were too far from it. The restaurant was a large log building that looked older than the other buildings around it, as if the town had built up around the place.

I walked around the car to meet Zachary, who waited for me on the cement walk that lined the front of the building. There were low bushes between the log walls and the cement walk. A few steps away was a large, covered patio with a few people seated out on the benches.

"Only the locals know how great this place is, and how popular," Zachary said, glancing at the people seated. "I made reservations."

It was cool inside and there was music coming from what was obviously a bar. It wasn't too loud but seemed loud after all the silence I'd had at Kernroote. The place smelled heavenly of steak and garlic and something fried, probably fish.

"Zachary!" The hostess was a pretty woman, about my age, dressed in a dark outfit that showed off a lot of leg. She clearly knew Zachary.

"Jenna," Zachary said. He didn't hold out a hand but he smiled. "It's good to see you. I didn't know you worked on Sundays."

"Normally I don't, but there was a last minute change," she said. "And I needed the money. Chloe has needs, you know." She laughed at that.

I wondered if Chloe was her daughter.

Zachary just nodded but didn't offer to introduce us. Either she wasn't as good of a friend as she made out or he lacked manners. I wondered which it was. He could be infallibly charming when he was at Kernroote acting the host, but other times, I wasn't so sure. It was as if he forgot I was there.

Jenna led us to a booth near a window without asking anything else. The place had a high, open ceiling with beams that ran the length of the place. The conversations created an ambient noise so that it was hard to hear the music in the background. The tables were a little too close together but they were well set with fine china on the pine tops. There were no tablecloths, just plaid placemats. It was a look that shouldn't have worked, but it did.

"Will this do?" she asked.

Zachary nodded and we slipped into the banquette. The seats were a nice black vinyl and the table was also pine. The backs were hard pine and they were raised above my head. There were carvings along the top of the wood which matched the carving that ran just below the window.

"They make some nice food here," Zachary said. "Brian likes to experiment so you never know what he might have. One day he might decide to do a barbeque duck or something really odd like that and the next day he might do a sirloin steak with mushroom sauce that's common everywhere."

The menus were paper and inside was a computer sheet with the day's specials. There was nothing fancy about any of it.

"He's got lamb chops today. That's my choice," Zachary said. "I've had these before and they're definitely his specialty."

"I'm not sure I've had lamb before," I said. I looked at the steaks, which seemed terribly expensive. I mean I've had filets before, but not at prices like that. I could go to the grocer and buy half a cow for that price if I shopped carefully.

"You must try it," Zachary told me. "Or maybe not. It will ruin you on lamb chops elsewhere forever."

I gave him a smile, setting the menu aside. It seemed as good of a time as any to try them and learn what the fuss about lamb was. I hadn't ever had it, wasn't sure I wanted to. Lambs, after all, were sweet creatures and here I was about to eat one when there were so many other choices. But then if I started thinking that I'd have to go through the ethics of eating all meat, because why should one creature live and another die just because I liked that creature?

"So tell me all about Becca Winter," Zachary said, reaching his hands across the table to take mine.

I wasn't sure I was ready for such an intimate gesture but I let him take my hand and told him a little about myself. He was a surprisingly good listener, and somewhere between ordering wine and the arrival of our dinner I was telling him about my divorce and my desire to write a novel.

"Romance?" he repeated. "Are you sure you came to the right place? I'd think my castle was much more about horror."

"Sometimes I think I've done the wrong thing too. Especially last night." I told him about the lights going out and the thundering from upstairs.

"Richard and his family know to be quiet when they're up there," Zachary said, frowning.

"Richard told me it was likely water in the pipes. You can't expect them not to drink water or use the toilet."

Zachary nodded, but there was something behind his eyes that said he wasn't mollified by my protests. I had unwittingly gotten Richard into trouble again.

"Does he have a large family, then?" I asked, trying to change the subject but not too abruptly. "Richard, I mean?"

"He has three boys. There's Cam, and then he has two younger sons. Richard's wife is a computer tech. Can you believe it?"

"Shouldn't I?" I asked.

"Richard just strikes me as so old-fashioned. Like his wife ought to hand sew clothing or take in mending like they did a hundred years ago. But no. She's a computer technician, one of the newer jobs out there." Zachary shook his head.

Our meals came and they smelled heavenly. I wasn't

sure what the spices were but there was something savory with a hint of a bite. And then there was the mint. A light sauce was draped over the chops and I wondered how that would work with the mint. Zachary was already tucking in to some root vegetables that were diced in large square portions.

I picked at the vegetables and tasted the sauce. It was wonderful, the spice exploding on my tongue but not over-whelming the rich savory flavor of it. It would be the perfect meal on a cold winter day. My body felt warmer than it had all evening already. And more relaxed, although I had to admit, it could have been the wine, a light-bodied red that I wasn't familiar with that went down a little too easily.

We continued talking about jobs and the things Zachary was interested in. I shouldn't put it like that. I was asking what he was interested beyond the hotel business and what had made him decide to create a hotel. And why not a resort?

"It's too hilly up there for golf. The Biltmore had a large swath of flat land. I guess I could purchase more land around the place and have horses and maybe put in a pool. I'd have to do another addition."

"I'm surprised you didn't add a pool to one of the first floor wings," I said. "And maybe a space for a spa."

"I'm not much of a spa guy myself." Zachary laughed. "And it seemed like I wanted space for people who couldn't make it upstairs. The ADA makes things hard for buildings as old as Kernroote…" He held up a hand. "I'm not dissing that. I know that not everyone is made the same. It's just that it's hard to retool an old place like that. I wanted plenty of places for people with less mobility."

I nodded. He certainly had his heart in the right place.

"But now that you mention it, people have asked

about a pool and I just have the hot tub indoors. I could do a large glassed-in area on the far side of the wing by the garage. The rooms there aren't done. I have the plans but they can be scrapped. I could even leave in the glass doors that are there and people could go out and sit outside. Maybe the other side can become almost all windows or I could build out a windowed area for the pool. I've seen images of roofs you can roll back for when it's warm."

He seemed enthusiastic about the idea.

"What sorts of things do spas have?" He was once again looking at me.

I told him what I had heard of but knew it wasn't an inclusive list. It wasn't like I went to high end spas of the sort I pictured for Kernroote. I tend to be careful with money. Perhaps it's the manager in me. In fact, if I hadn't gotten a rate and if Kara hadn't been pushing me, I doubt if I'd have taken time to spend in a place like Kernroote just to write.

"I've considered those things, and I guess I just wanted to start on the hotel and get guests coming in. I am a businessman, even if I inherited everything, and I want things to be in the black. But now, I'm wondering if shouldn't have made Kernroote more of a destination in and of itself."

"That's sort of how it was advertised," I pointed out.

Zachary smiled. "So perhaps I was subconsciously thinking it was a destination in and of itself." We clinked glasses on that note.

Zachary ordered us crème brûleé for dessert. I wouldn't have gotten anything but he insisted. "It's divine."

And it was. There was the slightest hint of an orange spice in the vanilla, and all in all it was a perfect finish to a fine dinner.

"You should have hired your friend away for your restaurant," I told him.

"I tried," Zachary laughed. "But he thinks Kernroote is too creepy and he didn't want to work there."

As we walked out to the car, he unlocked the door but left me to open it for myself. So much for being the perfect gentleman. Of course, he hadn't opened the car door for me earlier. Perhaps I was wishing for something he didn't even know to offer. I wondered what he'd be like once we were back at the hotel. Nothing like dating the owner of the place you're staying in to make saying good night feel awkward.

The question was, what would I do if he acted as if he wanted to come up for something more intimate or if he asked me to his rooms for something more intimate? I wasn't at all certain that I wanted to take him up on that. Yes, he was attractive, but he annoyed me in many ways. There was something patronizing about the way he had talked about a pool. Yes, he was enthusiastic, but he'd certainly considered those things before and decided not to do them. I had no idea why and he was clearly not going to share that information with me.

He drove the Tesla quickly back along the side roads. I kept up my end of the conversation but Zachary was surprisingly quiet. I gave up when we neared the gate of Kernroote.

"These were used once," he said. "We used to open and close the gates when I was growing up. Richard was concerned about leaving them open to the public when I wanted to make this a hotel."

"It isn't as safe," I said.

Zachary shook his head. "No. It's not."

He said nothing more, guiding the car expertly around the roads that led to the castle and at a much faster speed than I was comfortable with. The Tesla might handle well, but what would we do if another car came around the curve at the wrong time?

But we made it without incident and Zachary pulled around the side to go into the garage.

Richard was waiting for us, coming through the door as if he'd been looking out to catch Zachary when he came home.

Chapter 13

"Richard," Zachary said, getting out of the car.

I started to open the door but Richard was there, opening it, holding out a hand for me to take. He certainly had manners but perhaps that was because it was his job. He certainly didn't look at me as if he were friendly at all.

"I'm sorry," Richard said, clearly speaking to Zachary and not to me. "But I was talking to Cam about the problems on the fifth floor yesterday and I realized that perhaps there was a bit more noise than there needed to be."

Zachary raised an eyebrow at him. The two men stared at each other. I was certain that had I not been there, the conversation would have gone much differently.

"I have taken the liberty of moving Ms. Winter to the second floor. The suite there has a balcony and is nicer even than the room she's staying in. No one has reserved it for the rest of her stay," Richard said.

He was still talking to Zachary.

"I can go pack my stuff, then, before I settle in," I said.

"I took the liberty of having Cam do it," Richard said.

"I had some trouble with that fuse while you were out this evening and I didn't know when you'd be returning." His eyes never left Zachary's face.

I looked to Zachary. He didn't look pleased. I suppose the suite that Richard talked about was a special one. I hated that I might be causing trouble between them.

"You really should have texted me, Richard."

"You gave me the job of running the day-to-day activities of the hotel." Richard was still glaring at Zachary as if Zachary was a naughty boy.

"Very well," Zachary said finally.

He walked around the car. I was standing by the closed door, near Richard who hadn't moved since helping me out of the car.

I waited for some indication of what Zachary wanted me to do. He looked at me for a long moment and then nodded. I followed him to the door. Richard waited until we had passed and then he followed us.

"Stop by the desk," Richard told me. "I'll get you your new key."

"You didn't bother to make one up?" Zachary asked, clearly exasperated.

"I didn't think..." Richard trailed off, saying nothing more.

Zachary glared at him. We all trooped down the hallway. Any romance that might have been was gone for the evening. While Richard's forgetting to make a key and meeting us in the garage like a watchful father might have put a damper on things, the real reason any romance had left was Zachary himself.

It was quiet in the lobby, as always. It wasn't the near silence that I had become accustomed to, though. There were clearly other people around. Perhaps the place only got busy during the evening hours, like a hotel for vampires, which was so not where I needed my mind to go in this place.

"I've moved you to room 218," Richard said. "I'll take you there."

"I'm sure I can find it," Zachary said, with a tight smile for Richard. Richard, to his credit, just nodded and gave me the key, although Zachary had held out his hand.

"The Wi-Fi password is the same on all floors," Richard said, without looking at either of us. He was bent over something at the desk.

"Thank you," I said, and turned.

"It's easiest to go up the stairs, I think," Zachary said. "Of course, what do I know? I just lived here and designed the place." He raised his voice at the end to be sure that Richard heard. He was acting like a petulant child.

I almost wanted to tell him I could find my own way, but I worried that would make things worse for Richard. While I hadn't liked the desk clerk, at least he'd been decent to me. Besides, while disapproving, he seemed to want to be fair about things and he clearly cared about the customers.

I followed Zachary up the stairs, moving quickly because he walked so fast. He turned away from the restaurant so we crossed the catwalk over the lobby. I walked through a large loft area where the rock from the downstairs fireplace reached up through. It was a secluded little spot with an angled window. I imagined being curled up there with a book on a snowy evening. While it was certainly too early for snow, it might be a nice place to write.

Zachary didn't pause, although I would have, when I noticed that there were books along those shelves. We hurried around and passed the elevators on the second floor. We walked around another little jog in the corridor and this time, Zachary paused before a door. It was at an odd angle, facing out in the inward corner of the jog. When we went inside, I saw that was because of how the place was laid out. There was a large, almost round entry. To my right was a small kitchen, although there was still no stove. Beyond that was a sitting area, much larger than one I had had. It had two club chairs in white leather and a sofa in cream-and-blue fabric. The carpet was the same gray and green, but the walls in this room were a cheery cream.

There was a wall between the seating area and the sleeping area. I had to walk in a bit further. The door on my left was a bathroom that looked even larger than the one I had had. The sleeping area, when I got to it, was also larger. The bed faced a television, but there was also a sliding glass door next to the television that led out to a balcony at least partially covered by the floor of the room above.

"It's huge," I said.

"It does seem a little overdone sometimes. I wasn't happy with the colors on the sofa," Zachary said. "I had hoped the blue would have blended with the carpet a bit better but this was one of my early efforts. There's one like this on the fifth floor, although if Richard insists that it's too noisy up there on bad days I'm not sure I'll ever get him to rent it out."

"I'm sure you'll work something out," I said, turning.

Zachary took a look around. He moved something from a table that was near the door. I didn't see what it was but it appeared red. I couldn't think of anything I owned that would have been a problem.

"Thank you for dinner," I finally said, lamely. I had no idea what to do. It wasn't as if I could invite him in for wine.

"Thank you," Zachary said, smiling finally, remembering his manners. "I'm sorry it ended as it did."

"Well, it will all work out, I'm sure." I was pleased that Richard had finally moved me, although it would have been nice if he'd said something sooner and let me help.

Zachary gave me a long, awkward look. We could have been thirteen-year-olds trying to decide if we should kiss or not. I didn't move towards him. I didn't want to encourage him to think he could stay any longer. I wanted to make sure all my things were there.

Finally he nodded and left. I locked the dead bolt after him and set the security chain. I sighed and then went looking for the closet, which turned out to be off the bathroom, a larger walk-in than my parents had at their house. As far as I could tell, everything I brought was there. My computer was in the sitting area, not on the coffee table like I'd left it in the other room but on a desk near one of the club chairs. It was plugged in and charging.

I appreciated the thought. No doubt Cam understood how important it was to be connected, at least virtually, to the outside world, given his age. I looked in drawers and in the refrigerator. Everything seemed to be there and as close to where I had left it as possible.

I yawned, surprised. But it was getting late and the sun was setting, leaving a slight pink to the gray-looking clouds. I turned on all the lights. There were still shadows but they didn't seem as dense as those on the fifth floor. I decided it would be a good time to curl up and do some reading, maybe with the television on. My fifth-floor experiences hadn't completely left me.

When I couldn't keep my eyes open any longer, I curled up on the bed, which was every bit as comfortable as the one upstairs, and fell asleep easily. I thought perhaps I'd dream of Zachary but instead I dreamed of the fifth floor.

I dreamed I was running down the hallway in the wing near my room. The hallway was narrower and more shadowed than anything I'd seen during the day. The shadows weren't actually shadows but limbs of a tree that was trying to eat me. The mouth, I knew, was far below the surface but if it caught me, I'd be forced down there.

I was nearly caught when Zachary showed up in the hallway, rescuing me. Except then he was caught by the branches and I started awake as he was being carried down through the floor to be fed to the monster tree.

Laying on the bed, I shivered, glad I had left on some lights. I had turned off the lights in the sitting room but I'd left everything in the bedroom on. I'd hoped that I'd feel comfortable turning lights off again the next night but now I doubted I'd ever want to sleep in the dark.

I got up to grab a glass of water, looking around, searching for shadows, but the room was fairly benign-looking. My heartbeat slowed back to a more normal level as I drank the water, trying to piece together the dream. It was definitely strange.

I heard someone go running down the hallway. Quick thumping feet, too fast to be someone walking, and I wondered who was out there. At least there were people, I thought. It was better to have sounds than nothing, as I'd had on the fifth floor.

Something scratched at the window as I started to climb into bed. It sounded like a tree branch on glass might sound. There were firs outside my apartment and sometimes in the wind those branches scratched at the glass. Except, I realized that there was a balcony and no tree close enough. I sat up, staring to my right where the window was, wanting to get up and look out through the curtains I had pulled but not daring to do so.

With the lights on, I reminded myself, I would see

nothing out there. To see anything, I would have to turn off the lights. That did it. I huddled under the covers, pulling them up over my head like a child, and tried to go to sleep. I drifted and dozed but I heard water gurgle in the pipes, thankfully a gurgle and not the thundering that it was upstairs, and the faint hum of the air conditioner. The building seemed to groan when it settled and now and then there was the faintest sound of scratching. All normal enough sounds, except, perhaps, for the scratching.

I started to drift off when the smell came. It was the same skunk smell that I'd noticed in the garden. The windows weren't open so I wondered where it came from. Was there a plant that smelled that bad or were there skunks around that just kept dying? I had no idea. I covered my nose as best I could and tried to breathe through my mouth.

I must have drifted off because the next thing I knew there was light slipping under the curtains.

Chapter 14

I looked for Zachary at breakfast but he wasn't around. I grabbed one of my favorite tables towards the back of the room near the window. Chris, who would always be the gray-eyed man in my personal set of nicknames, was finishing up on the other side of the room. He came over to say good morning.

"Do you have plans today?" he asked.

"I'm hoping to do a bit of work, writing," I said.

He smiled then, nodding. "I had no idea you were a writer. What an exciting vocation."

I gave him a smile back, not sure. He seemed to want to sit down, but I wasn't interested in talking more to him. I was grumpy after my disastrous date with Zachary.

"I was just going to do some hiking today around the area. There are some marvelous trails and things."

"I hope that the weather holds for it," I said.

Chris nodded, glancing around. He shifted his weight a little as if he hoped I'd invite him to sit down—I couldn't put my finger on why I had no desire to encourage him—

but I didn't. Perhaps it was just a small, mean-spirited part of me that wanted to see if he'd give in and ask or perhaps just sit himself down.

Instead, he wished me a good day and left.

Which left me vaguely disappointed and wondering what had gotten into me. Probably all the nightmares that I'd been having, not to mention Zachary's grumpy mood.

When I left the breakfast room I saw Richard at the desk. No one was checking in and the room was its usual silent self, but there was Richard, working away. He glanced up, looking at me from below his heavy eyebrows and nodded just a little. The disapproving look never left his face.

I went around the corner to use the elevator. Going up the stairs seemed like it just gave me a long walk around the lobby for no good reason. I might as well take the elevator. I nearly pressed five by mistake but corrected that before I had to ride all the way up and then back down. My hands were sweating at the thought and I considered forcing myself to go up and come back down just to prove that it wasn't terrible, but I couldn't make myself do it.

On the second floor I decided to go wandering. I went down the hallway towards the room that was in roughly the same place as the room I was in on the fifth floor. The numbers were approximately the same, probably for ease of use of the staff. The hall wasn't any wider but it seemed brighter.

The paintings here were of flowers in the green and pink colors that were in the lobby. It was pleasant enough. There was the faintest smell of disinfectant and something like rosemary, but that could have come from the kitchen. Still, it was a nice change from the complete neutrality of the fifth floor.

I heard a television on in a room on the right, letting me know that there were people around. I was so thrilled I was tempted to knock just to see another guest, but I pushed that impulse aside. I made my way to the end of the corridor and turned left onto the wing that, on the fifth floor, was unfinished.

Things were further along here. There were still fluorescent bulbs in the ceiling and the hall was still too narrow, but the walls were cream and the wall on my right, just before the first door, had a collage of photos of the hotel. It was in black and white but was clearly modern as it showed people working on the rooms in the hotel.

I saw an image of Cam mugging for the camera as he helped carry in some carpet. That surprised me. I would have thought that you'd have carpet layers who just came in and did the work on their own. Then I saw Zachary showing a woman around the place. She had dark hair like Zachary and she was beautiful, with dark eyes and a trim, lithe figure. She smiled brightly and seemed entranced by all he was saying as they toured the place. There was even a photo of them in the garden where she looked disturbed by something, and I couldn't help but think of the dead pond that I'd been seeing.

Clearly they were working together on the castle. There was one other shot where they were talking and the woman was looking at something off camera, a slight frown pulling the skin between her eyebrows into a tight wrinkle. I wondered what she'd seen behind the cameraman. I moved on down the hall and saw that while there were some images of flowers in the same color scheme—a hundred different takes of the same still life—there were other collages.

I paused at the next one. This was clearly older. Again

the images were in black and white. The people there were dressed like people in the 1950s or so, and a man who might have been Zachary's grandfather was showing around a group of people. They were in the garden and then in the lobby, which was just a large formal entry, like a castle hall. It was darker there, with only near black, dark gray, and some faintly lighter gray. I practically had to press my nose against the photo to see anything.

Another image showed a large bedroom. I had no idea where it was but it clearly wasn't one of the rooms in the hotel, although perhaps it was where Zachary had gotten the idea. It had a huge four-poster bed that took up almost the entire room and there was a grand set of French doors that looked off onto a balcony, the curtains blowing inward, so the window was clearly open.

I shook my head. How very interesting to see the history of the place. The next set, which was almost down at the end of the hall wing, was older still. This one included the man that at first I took to be Richard. Looking at the clothing it was clear it was not, but it was equally clear that it was a family member. This man didn't quite have the disapproval on his face that was etched into Richard's. Instead he looked wary.

He was in a large dining room, a room I hadn't seen. It looked over the garden and from the angle, I thought it was probably on the first floor, somewhere near where the current kitchens likely sat, assuming they were close to both the breakfast room and the restaurant upstairs.

The dining room was all mahogany paneled and even had a tapestry of hunting scenes falling from the edges of a two-story ceiling. There was a rail around the upper part of the room so that people could sit or stand on the balcony. I wondered if the Kernrootes had once been known for parties.

I got to the end of that hallway. I opened the door to the stairwell. It opened easily. It was strange that I could open the door on this side but not the other side. I held the door open to look out to see if there were a place for a key. There was a knob that turned on both sides of the door so it shouldn't have been locked the other day. I had no desire to go running through the basement again, so I backed out and let the door close.

I decided I wanted to know more about the history of the house, so I walked quickly back down the hallway and around the corner. The television was still on in the one room. I felt much more at home. A more normal hotel experience than the one I'd had on the fifth floor.

I crossed over to my part of the building and considered walking down the other wing, but thought I had enough to do keep me occupied for some time. No doubt the castle had plenty of history for me to go through and when I was done, I could do some more writing.

My suite had been made up and everything looked in place. It smelled faintly of cleaning products. It made me wonder if there was a better air filtration system or vent upstairs. I'd never noticed such a thing on the fifth floor. I wouldn't worry about it, I told myself. Both rooms were cleaned.

I went over the sitting area. It was darker in that part of the room, although there was a big window that looked out over the garden. In fact, I was probably almost right above the same spot I'd looked out from downstairs in the breakfast room. I saw Zachary come out of the garden with the dark-haired woman who had appeared in the photos. It was almost as if having seen her, I had conjured her.

They didn't seem chummy, really, and as they walked I

thought I noticed a family resemblance, but that could have been my mind searching for it.

At any rate, I was definitely going to have to search out more on the Kernroote family. There was a lot Zachary wasn't telling me, not that he needed to, really, but now I was nosy.

<hr>

Chapter 15

<hr>

I settled in and waited for the computer to connect to the Internet. It seemed to go slower in this room. I wondered if it was all the cement and brick of the building that kept the Wi-Fi from working so well.

I finally got connected, though there were people on old dial-up systems who would have connected faster. Fortunately I'm not an Internet junkie and if I really had a hard time, I determined that I'd go find a Starbucks or a library where I could do my research. In fact, I might even get better Wi-Fi if I were in my car out in the parking lot.

I put in Kernroote as a search term. The hotel had an advertised listing in the search engine but the other listings appeared to include the history of the castle and information about the family. I looked up the history of the castle first.

Zachary was right in that no one knew how old the place was. One site said there were legends that the castle had been there before the first white settlers had arrived in the area.

The tribal nations had been known to give the area a

wide berth. They had legends of a large tree imprisoned in giant cave, which I suppose could have been a stone building. Of course, what did that mean? Had it been built by aliens along with Stonehenge? While all of this was an interesting, intellectual pursuit, it told me nothing of value and not what I really wanted to understand, not that I could have put my finger on what exactly that was.

I looked up the family next. It was frustrating to sit drumming my fingers, wondering if anything was going to show up in the search while the computer and the Internet talked slowly together. After a couple of minutes the search results finally began to show up. I clicked on several of them.

The Kernroote family was an old family that had been in the area forever. They had always lived on the land that housed the castle. In the first article it was suggested that they had lived on the land for a long time but had built the castle in more modern times. Based on what Zachary had told me, the building that had gone on could have been referring to the expansion that included the wings that ran along each side of the main building.

The current heir was Zachary Kernroote and there was a nice photo of him. His next of kin was Naomi Kerne. She was a year younger than Zachary and was the daughter of Zachary's father's sister. Naomi had grown up with Zachary as her mother had been in and out of rehab.

While Zachary was considered a savvy businessman and was devoted to making Kernroote Castle a destination in the North Carolina mountains, Naomi was considered something of a player.

She worked in IT but was anything but a typical nerd. She had sold one of her software security packages to a large conglomerate at a young age and in addition to her family's portion of the Kernroote fortune, she had made her own. Now she worked on projects that interested her.

There were plenty of rumors about her and Zachary. Some suggested that they were lovers, rather like an Egyptian dynastic marriage, though they weren't actual brother and sister, merely cousins. Others said they had had a falling out over the management of the Kernroote estate, the literal castle part of the estate.

The image of Naomi suggested she was definitely the woman who was wandering the garden with Zachary. They hadn't looked like two people who had had a falling out, though there had been a coolness about their posture in the photo I had seen, but who knew? Perhaps they only saw each other on rare occasions because of Naomi's opinion of the hotel. I had no idea.

It was interesting, though.

I looked up more information on Zachary, even going to Facebook to see if he listed himself there and whether he was in a relationship. He didn't have a profile, but Kernroote had a page. Naomi also had a profile but wasn't listed as being in a relationship. I hated that I was sleuthing about, trying to find out if Zachary was romantically interested in Naomi. It suggested I was much more interested in him than I wanted to admit.

I put the computer away and stood up and stretched. I walked out to the balcony and wondered if I should go for a walk in the garden. The skunk smell reached my nose and I decided that if I went for a walk, it wouldn't be there. I sighed. I needed to call Kara and tell her what I knew, but I was reluctant to tell her about my date with Zachary. It had gone so badly. Kara, no doubt, would have found a way to cajole Zachary into being in a better mood no matter what had happened.

After stretching, I decided I would go for that walk, just

not in that garden. After all, Chris of the gray eyes had said there were plenty of trails.

I went downstairs and out the front. Richard was gone from the desk, which didn't surprise me at all. I walked down through the parking lot and then off to the side of the road that came down the last hill. There was the faintest trail off the left of the road and I walked along there up the clear hillside where I could look back at Kernroote and then down into the trees.

It was cooler under the trees and the path diverged from the road not far after that. It was a pleasant enough walk that felt as if it were circling Kernroote Castle. The air was fresh and the cicadas were humming. There were birds flitting from tree to tree calling to each other. It was a longish walk that circled back to the back side of the castle, forcing me to walk down the walkway that ran beside the formal garden, where things quieted down, but until that point everything had been completely normal.

I can't say that anything unusual happened near the garden except I heard a few skitterings in the bushes like a chipmunk or other small creature was moving around in there. I peered into an entrance on that side and saw nothing odd about the place. Perhaps all of that had been my imagination. Perhaps paint fumes or fumes from the construction in the west wing of the castle had gotten to me and I had been hallucinating odd things.

I smiled at the thought before I headed up to the room to get a little writing done before I went out to find some lunch. After running those errands, I felt refreshed and ready to tackle more of my book. I practically bounced into the lobby and nearly ran into Chris.

Chapter 16

"I'm sorry!" he cried, backing up. "I should watch where I'm going. Everyone tells me I'm always lost in thought."

"No. I shouldn't have been running inside." I moved back to a more comfortable distance. Chris made me feel vaguely uncomfortable, but I wasn't sure why. Of course, perhaps it was because I couldn't read him. His gray eyes always seemed so cool and in control that I enjoyed it when his body betrayed that he wasn't quite so confident.

"No, that's fine," Chris said. "It looks like you had a good walk. Were you in the garden?"

"Not today," I answered. "I thought about what you said about the trails and I found a path just to the left of the road out front."

Chris nodded. "I walked that. It wasn't a very long walk, but pleasant. Very different from trying to find your way through the maze out there. I've heard that some people get lost in the garden maze."

"I thought perhaps I had the first day," I said. "But I was rescued and found my way out."

The dark-haired woman that I had seen in the garden with Zachary glided out from the breakfast room.

"Good afternoon," she said pleasantly. She was a pretty woman but her shoulders were broad like a man's and her face almost too symmetrical to be beautiful.

"Good afternoon," Chris said. He moved so that he stood almost between me and the woman I suspected was Naomi Kerne. I wanted to shove him out of the way but wasn't sure how to do so without being rude.

"Have you found our gardens?" she asked.

Chris nodded. "I had no problem with the maze at all the other day. Becca, however, said she needed to be rescued."

Naomi gave me a long look. "Really?"

"Richard came and found me," I said.

A troubled look crossed Naomi's face. "Perhaps staying to the wooded trails would be better. While long-distance hikers get lost, the paths close to the castle are clearly marked and always come out somewhere inhabited."

Chris had moved just enough that I could see his reaction, which seemed overly excited at her comments. "Do you mean to say people actually have been lost in the maze?"

Naomi looked at him again, then seemed to dismiss him. "Oh, I think it would just look bad for Zachary if a guest got lost in the garden and couldn't find her way out. So much better to be a lost hiker, don't you think? I'm so mercenary that way." She laughed then as if that lightened her comment.

It made me shiver; the laugher almost worse than the comment itself.

Chris didn't seem to know what to say either, nodding, his jaw tensing and clenching as if he was wondering how to phrase a new question.

Naomi headed him off. "Enjoy your stay. My cousin will be so pleased to know that romance finds people in the castle. He can add it to his website." She didn't smile when she said that, as if she didn't think Zachary would like any such thing.

Chris turned to me when she had left us behind. "Well, that was interesting."

I nodded. "I guess I'd better not ruin the atmosphere by dying lost in the maze."

He laughed then, an easy laugh. "Actually, you'll probably think I'm crazy, but there have been rumors the place is haunted. I came here hoping to find a ghost."

I raised an eyebrow. I hadn't come upon that in my research.

Chris reddened a little, his fair skin making it easy to do. He looked down and scuffed his foot like a young boy before bidding me a good afternoon. He walked around to the elevator while I headed up the stairs.

I walked around the second floor catwalk, looking down into the lounge that seemed further away than it was. I held on to the rail, feeling momentarily dizzy. When it passed, I hurried towards my room, completely forgetting to examine the books in the cozy little reading alcove.

I opened my room door only to find the place in complete shadow. I tried to tell myself it was a normal shadowy darkness because the lights were out, except, on second glance, the lights were on as I'd left them. I stepped back, not certain what to do, unsure how the room came to be so dark. I smelled the scent of fresh pine, as if I were in a forest. The smell was gone as quickly as it came.

The room lightened and I breathed again.

I still hesitated at the threshold.

"Is there a problem?" Zachary asked, walking down

the hall. He was coming from the western part of the castle, the wing I hadn't yet explored.

"No. The room just looked dark for a moment," I said.

He paused and looked inside and then at me. "It can take some time for your eyes to adjust to the light."

"It was that, I'm sure," I said.

"And just a reminder, we do like it when guests turn off their lights when they leave." It was said with a smile, as if he were only saying it to make conversation and not as a reprimand.

"I go out on the balcony and things are so bright that it's easy to miss the lights when I come in." I had no idea why I felt a need to lie to him about not wanting to be in the room when it was dark.

"Of course," Zachary said. There was still a smile and a hesitation as if he wanted to say something more.

Finally he spoke again. "I'm sorry I missed you at breakfast. I had some family things to attend to. My cousin just came in from out of town, which always messes up my schedule. I usually help out at breakfast during the week."

"It would have been lovely to have a chat," I said. "But I certainly don't expect that you'll drop all your duties as hotelier just to entertain me."

Zachary nodded. "Perhaps if it works out, tomorrow we could explore the garden again. This time without the rain. There's more there that I could show you. Or, if you prefer, we could explore one of the trails that winds around the woods near the castle."

"I think I'd love to explore the trails," I said. Perhaps that was foolish but I had no desire to see the garden again. Ever. I also didn't feel completely comfortable putting Zachary off, either. I couldn't put my finger on why. It might just have been some lingering physical attraction that had, unfortunately, not been acted on.

Zachary gave me a large smile, almost relieved, and then told me he would see me after breakfast ended, around ten-thirty tomorrow. I agreed and entered the room. It no longer looked so shadowy. I sniffed, trying to pick up a hint of pine. Perhaps the cleaners had used a pine cleanser, but the smell was gone, with only the faintest traces of bleach under the fading, rather acrid smells of new carpet and paint.

I went into the sitting room and settled at my computer. I was surprised to see the screen was on and my word processor was open. I picked it up and looked at it. The words read like mine except the last paragraph, which said, "The gray-eyed man wasn't at all what she thought he was. Instead he was a spy, a thief, a killer. He stood in the entry to the room, holding a knife, ready to take care of her in the way only he could."

I pushed the screen away and stood up. I walked two quick steps to the entry area and looked around. No one stood there. I drew in a breath. The room smelled ordinary. I heard only the beat of my heart. There was the faintest hiss as the air conditioning came on. Everything else was still.

I looked in the bathroom and walked through there to the walk-in closet. Nothing. I even searched behind my clothing.

I walked back out to the bedroom. My bed hadn't been touched. I saw no one. One corner of the bed skirt twitched and I drew in a hitched breath. My heart started to pound even more loudly.

I got down on my hands and knees, slowly, keeping an eye on the bed skirt, which didn't move again. I stared at it, willing whatever was under there to part the cloth and come out, but the skirt remained still. I was breathing too hard. I had no idea if I'd watched the bed skirt for thirty seconds or if I'd been there an hour. My heart needed a break. I was no doubt aging years in these few days.

I flicked the skirt aside. There was only a long black base beneath the bed. Nothing had been under there. The air from the vent in the ceiling was hitting me, so perhaps it had hit the skirt at just the right angle as I'd watched.

I felt silly, but no calmer. I stood up and went out on the balcony, checking all corners. No one there. No one was even out in the garden, not that I blamed them.

I stood listening to the birds for long enough to have sweat bead on my forehead. The afternoon felt close and still, like a storm was coming, although, as yet, there were no clouds. Everything was just waiting.

I should pack up my stuff and just leave, I thought. But I hated to give up. If I went home, would I be able to write? I doubted it. Besides, I couldn't just kick out my renters. They were there for three months. Mentally I listed all the things I'd have to do to go home.

I needed a vacation from my vacation.

If I picked up the phone and called Richard, would he be of help? Or was he the person who had been in my room?

Zachary had been at the other end of the hall, but what was he doing on the second floor?

Either of them, or perhaps Cam, could have left that note. I bit my lip, worrying it between my teeth as I thought.

If I left, would I ever learn the answers? If I left, would I really be free or would one of them stalk me even after that? It was a strange note. If they meant me harm, why not just try and hurt me? Why try to panic me into running?

I thought about the winding drive that led to the castle. A car accident wouldn't be uncommon there. I could easily be injured. Far more difficult to injure me in the hotel and not have the hotel itself be questioned. That would hurt business.

If it was Richard or Zachary, that could be a motive. But why would Zachary show himself in the hallway then? If he hadn't been there at all I'd never have known. That still left me with Richard.

There was also, I thought, the outside chance that it was someone like Cam or someone I hadn't even met who didn't like me. But the interesting thing was that they had used the nickname I'd given Chris just when Chris and I had started talking a bit more. I hadn't mentioned it to anyone. It gave me a chill to think that someone knew what it was.

I paced around the room, trying to calm myself. No one was in the room with me. I had set the privacy lock. It wasn't much, but at least I'd have warning if someone tried to break in. I tried calling my sister but naturally it went to voicemail.

After much pacing, I made myself go into the sitting room. My computer was still where I had set it aside. It had taken all my effort not to toss the thing away after reading the last line. I picked it up and set it on the table. I was worried about touching it, as if it could somehow bite me. I hit the keys to bring it back.

And there was my work.

But that final line, the one that had troubled me, was gone.

Chapter 17

What was happening? Was I going crazy? I tried to find older versions of the document in the word processor but none of them showed the words I had read. Now I really needed to talk to Kara. She was a nurse. She could tell me if this was stress or something from my divorce and I was making it all up. I started to cry.

Once the tears started, I couldn't stop them. I was afraid of what was happening. I was worried. I had no idea what to do and not a clue who to turn to for help. I was certain I wasn't imagining these things so how could I go out and just act as if nothing had happened? I wasn't that good of an actress.

I couldn't just start asking Richard and Zachary questions. Even asking Cam about things like this seemed too much. I could probably ask Chris, considering he'd confessed to being a ghost hunter. Of course, would he actually believe me as I had no proof? And would he ascribe these things to a ghost rather than to some human hand that was trying to frighten me?

Though I hated not having proof of what I'd seen, I

was also relieved that the words were gone. Now I didn't have to deal with them. I just had to question my sanity.

My thoughts went around in circles while I cried myself out. Finally, my sobs subsided, but when they began to subside and I could see again, the pink sky was beginning to darken the sitting room. My head and eyes ached from the crying and I felt stiff. The poor pillow I had grabbed was as wet as if it had gotten left out in a rainstorm.

Fortunately Kernroote provided plenty of tissues and I went through them liberally as I tried to get myself back on track. I saved the document and closed the computer. I picked up the writing pad, that little half page memo pad hotels give you, and a Kernroote Castle pen. I scribbled on the top page to see if the ink worked. It did. The pen felt surprisingly good in my hand. I should have known. Kernroote appeared to spare no expense on little luxuries no one would notice.

I sat down to write. I listed the names of the men I suspected. Zachary, Richard, Cam, and even Chris. I thought for a moment and then I added Naomi. Then I listed where they were for each incident. Only Richard had been around for everything. Naomi hadn't been around at all, at least that I knew of, until today. I wasn't sure of the whereabouts of either Zachary or Chris.

Tomorrow, when I walked with Zachary—and foolish as it might be, I intended to go walking with him—I'd see if I could find out what had brought Naomi to Kernroote.

I considered going to have dinner, hoping to run into Zachary, but I suspected I'd look like I'd spent the afternoon crying, which wouldn't make me a very desirable companion to talk with. I could try to play on his sympathies but I had no idea if he had them. His emotions seemed far too changeable.

I was just starting to feel better, now that I had a plan, when my phone rang. I grabbed it, seeing it was Kara.

"What's up?" Kara didn't bother with a greeting when I answered. She went right to the point. That meant she was on break at work.

"This place is too weird," I said. "Do you have time or are you on break?"

"I grabbed a quick break. I'm done in a couple of hours, if the nurse on the next shift shows. Want me to call then?"

"When do you work tomorrow?" I asked.

"Day again. But then I have two days off." I could hear the smile in the voice. Kara might like her job but she loved her personal time as well.

"Call me then, okay?"

"Sure you'll be fine?"

"Yeah. I worked a lot of it out myself," I said.

"Good girl."

Hanging up the phone, I was aware of just how alone I was once again. Most of my friends were friends through work. Daniel and I had had couple-friends but not one-on-one friends. I stayed in touch with one couple, but mostly our friends had gone with Daniel when we divorced. I was surprised that Lisa and Rob had remained in contact. Of all our friends, I knew them the least and had thought they didn't particularly like me.

Despite the fact that I continued to get invitations to their events and often attended, this wasn't the type of thing I could chat about with Lisa. Which meant I had no one to talk to.

I mentally made a note to make more friends, people that I liked for things outside of work. I had to stop isolating, which made me laugh at myself considering I was holed up in a weird castle-hotel on the edge of nowhere. How much more isolated could I get?

I decided a shower was in order. I appreciated that this bathroom had a light connected to the fan, directly over the shower, so that it was bright in that part of the bathroom. The lights in the bathroom, both over the sink and the main one over the tub, also made the whole room plenty bright. I didn't have to worry about shadows. At least not there.

I took a very long shower with hot water to ward off the shivers I was feeling.

When I was done my head still ached but not like it had. My eyes didn't feel half-glued together. My thoughts even seemed clearer.

I had a plan. I wanted to write something but I didn't want to touch the computer. Instead, I opened it, closed out the word processor and turned it off. Maybe tomorrow there would be space between me and that line of text and I could go back to writing.

If I were truly rich, I thought, I could just go out and buy a new computer. I flipped through shows on the television. I considered dinner but the scare I'd had and the crying had crushed any appetite I might have. In fact, I felt vaguely nauseated.

When my eyelids started to droop, I got up and turned the lights off in the sitting area and then I crawled into bed. I did not turn the lights off in the bedroom, nor did I turn off the television.

I dropped off and had nightmares about faceless men slipping into my room and stealing my computer. In one particularly vivid dream, Zachary had stolen my romance story and sold it to a publisher. I hadn't known any of this until I found it on the shelf in a little bookstore. I was reading it and realizing that this was my story, not his. I started screaming in the store, unable to control myself, and I woke up when the manager yelled at me about being a baby.

I giggled a little, which felt good. It was still dark outside, so I curled up further into the blankets and tried to sleep. The television was on with the volume low but for some reason it sounded louder than it had been. I looked at the screen, not surprised to see a black-and-white movie on. It was clearly a suspense movie, I gathered from listening to the sound reel. A man in a dark suit was walking slowly down a path through what appeared to be a cave. There were roots of trees all over the place but sometimes they would reach out and try and grab him. He never turned but he had something in his hand to cut the roots off.

I couldn't figure out what the movie was. I could feel my body reacting to the music though. I was getting more awake and more tense. The man just kept walking along, going very slowly. A hand reached out of the dirt but he avoided it. I saw he had a glass full of something dark and thick. Although I hadn't seen the rest of the movie, I suspected it was blood.

The man turned a corner and he was walking through a basement. It was set up frighteningly like the basement I had walked through at Kernroote. I didn't want to watch any more. I grabbed the remote control but when I tried to turn the television off, nothing happened. The man was still walking along, carrying his glass of blood. The music was building and I knew that something was going to happen soon. I hit the power button again and the screen flickered but didn't turn off. Finally it went off, just as the man jumped, not expecting to see what he saw. There was a woman lying in a puddle of blood, wearing what looked like a modern jogging suit. Her hair was like mine. The picture disappeared before he could turn her over.

I nearly hit the button to turn the television back on but I stopped myself. I didn't want to know. I curled up in the bed, burying my head in the pillow, like a child afraid of the dark. I had to leave this place. I was going crazy or it was driving me crazy. Maybe it was all the chemicals in the new construction and remodeling.

Maybe in the morning I would run away and Google information about chemically induced psychosis. Except, of course, I was meeting Zachary for a hike. I didn't want to offend him by running away without an explanation.

When I woke in the morning, I expected the television to have been turned off, but it was back on and a morning news anchor was quietly reading the news in my room.

I shook my head, not understanding how I could have been so certain I had woken up in the middle of the night and watched part of a movie. It must have been a dream, but it had felt so real. Even the pillows were lying where I had moved them while hugging them to my chest watching the thriller.

The only thing to suggest I hadn't woken up was the television, which should have been off. Perhaps I hadn't actually turned it off. Except I knew better. Whatever was happening, it was getting worse. Perhaps *I* was getting worse.

I got dressed but it was still early for breakfast. I decided to do some searching online. It wasn't about Kernroote Castle at all. This time I was searching out mental health and symptoms of things like schizophrenia. I had hoped to find something that told me I didn't have it, but unfortunately while being in my mid-thirties suggested I was on the old side for a first episode, I couldn't completely rule out the possibility.

I could be experiencing a psychotic break of some sort, no doubt caused by the stress of my husband leaving me, or that's what they would put on the intake sheet if I had to go in for hospitalization. I nearly cried again. It was one thing to think something was possible, it was another to find that it was very likely what was happening to me.

I sat staring into space, wondering what this meant for some time. Eventually I roused myself enough so that I could down to breakfast. Perhaps food would help ground me a little more.

I was meeting Zachary later because what if I wasn't having a psychotic break? What if there was something going on? I needed the information he could give me to help me understand what it was.

As I left the room, listening to the silence around me, broken unexpectedly by a man's laughter, I wondered how I would know if I were really asking normal questions or if I were going around spouting gibberish. Perhaps that's why Richard always looked so disapproving.

I came down the stairs, avoiding the elevator again, and saw Naomi leaning over the desk with Richard. Richard had a smile on his face. I had no idea the man could smile.

Naomi heard me on the steps, turning in time to see me go past

"Good morning," she said a little too cheerfully.

"You look rather peaked this morning," Richard said. "Would you rather I had someone send your breakfast to the room?"

"Oh no. Thank you." I was surprised at how solicitous he was. Perhaps Cam had hacked into the Internet and programmed that sentence to show up and disappear—kids could do that, couldn't they? But perhaps if that were the case, Richard was trying to make up for it without admitting guilt.

"Are you certain?" Naomi asked. "You really shouldn't take a chance with your health."

So both of them wanted me to stay around.

"I'm sure I'll be fine with a little coffee and breakfast. And then I'll have a lovely outdoor walk with Zachary, which should perk me up even more. I'm sure I've been locked away trying to write my book too much."

I watched for any looks, but both of them just nodded as if that was the most natural thing in the world.

"Leave it to my cousin to find a way to spend time with the single female guests. I guess that explains why he wanted to remodel this into a hotel. I couldn't imagine the work that would take," Naomi said, smiling.

I gave her an awkward smile.

She nodded and turned back to Richard. The smile was gone from Richard's face. He looked at me with his usual disapproving scowl, although I had to admit I thought there might be a hint of worry there in the lines that had formed between his eyebrows.

There was no reason for me to stay and listen, but I also felt that whatever they were talking about concerned me. The sense was so strong that the hairs on the back of my neck stood up as I crossed to the breakfast room.

This morning the place was completely empty, so I took my usual table. The girl from the first day was back and she took my order for cheese blintzes. I was pleased that the girl kept the coffee coming as well.

I was almost awake when Zachary brought out my cheese blintzes. They were served with fresh fruit and sausage links and the whole plate smelled heavenly.

"I see you've chosen the quiet time to breakfast," Zachary said. "We had a bit of a rush about half an hour ago but now everyone seems to be off doing their own thing."

"It's nice to have a bit of quiet," I said. I didn't add that I'd rather have a few people around so I didn't feel like the only guest in the place. Where were these people who had been down? Had they checked out already?

"Has your room still been noisy?" Zachary asked, concerned.

"Oh no. Not at all." If anything, it was too quiet, I thought, though I didn't say that aloud. "I just had a hard time sleeping last night. Too much thinking, I'm sure."

Zachary nodded at me, the smile gone. "I hope you aren't trying for an excuse to get out of our walk. I was looking forward to it."

"No, it's not that. I'm looking forward to being outside as well. I expect it will perk me up as much as the coffee, if it's not too hot outside already."

"The temperatures are supposed to be more mild today than they were yesterday."

"Great."

"I will see you later, then," Zachary said, bowing a little and leaving.

I watched him go. Sometimes he seemed so formal about things. He seemed much more at ease glad-handing strangers. Maybe he was shy or uncertain about people one-on-one. Maybe it was just awkwardness that made him seem like a jerk. I ate some of the blintzes, which were very good, melting in my mouth with just enough tartness to offset the otherwise sweet flavor.

I chewed slowly, wondering if I'd have the nice Zachary or the dark and brooding Zachary when we went for our walk.

Chapter 18

Zachary was right when he'd said it was more mild today than yesterday. There were fluffy white clouds in the sky and a nice breeze that kept it from feeling too warm. It was pretty much perfect, and I worried it might be chilly under the trees. He'd actually been prompt to this meeting, standing at the desk with Richard when I came down the stairs from the second floor. They'd been having a discussion that I couldn't quite hear but the tone seemed a bit heated.

"There you are!" Zachary had smiled at me, turning. I thought there might be a look of relief on his face. I wondered if he had worried that I wouldn't show up or if I'd come at an opportune moment for him to break it off with Richard.

"I hope I'm not late," I said. I had checked the time on my phone before leaving. I'd been prompt coming down. Just exactly on time as I'd gotten up to leave about a minute before our meeting. Surely I hadn't walked that slowly across the catwalk to the stairs.

"Not at all," Zachary said.

Richard nodded but said nothing. If anything, he looked even more disapproving, though he kept his heavy-lidded eyes lowered. I had a sense he was watching me even if he wouldn't look at me, like a spy not wanting to get caught. I shivered.

"Shall we?" I asked. "I'm looking forward to being outside." *And away from Richard*, although I didn't say that.

"Of course." Zachary gestured to me to precede him out the front of the building. The uniformed man from the first day was there, standing off to the side, looking at his phone. He thrust it into his pocket and straightened up when he saw us.

"Morning, Mr. Kernroote," he said. He practically saluted.

"Morning, Hal," Zachary said, smiling. He said nothing about the phone either way.

I said nothing, nor did Zachary. Our shoes kicked at the gravel as we walked across the parking lot. I smelled the fresh air, immediately feeling less gloomy than I had in the castle.

"He'll be back on the phone in no time," Zachary said in a low voice. "If I really cared…if I ever put him on shifts when we were busy, he'd probably have been fired by now."

I laughed. "He was on when I arrived but he did take my bags up to my room for me."

"He likes the tips. He hates that I don't work him on the weekends when there are more visitors. He wants more but he doesn't care enough. He hates having to be nice to people and gets short with folks if they interrupt him when he's texting or talking. Now and then he's fine, which is why he's still here." Zachary shrugged.

"There are always pros and cons of employees," I said.

"You have employees as a writer?" Zachary asked,

looking at me harder, as if by looking through me he could see the potentially famous person he had met.

"No. But in my day job, the one I left in order to write, I was a manager and I hired and fired a number of people. I even had to do a layoff once."

"That must have been hard." That last was said almost absently, as if he had no real interest in my prior work.

I hedged, giving a generalized commentary rather than something longer. I asked him whether he enjoyed hiking around here and what trails he might like. That did elicit some discussion as he appeared to genuinely like the outdoors.

It had only been in the last few years, since he'd inherited the castle, that he'd begun spending much more time inside. By this time we'd reached the trail that I'd taken the day before and Zachary led me down it.

I was a tad disappointed that it appeared to be the same trail but it had been a pleasant enough walk. It was cool beneath the trees and there was plenty of shade—ordinary shade and not the shadows of the castle, or worse, the castle garden. Cicadas started their humming and then faded away like an orchestra ending its performance only to start on a new piece. A bird chirped and leaves rustled from small creatures scurrying in the underbrush.

Conversation turned to the relative merits of different parts of western Carolina. Zachary liked his home but preferred the mountains up near Boone. I liked the southwestern part of the state. "And the beach," I added. "I like the beach too."

"What made you decide to come to the mountains instead?" he asked. This time he sounded genuinely curious.

"My sister told me about Kernroote and it looked more interesting than one of the more standard hotels along the coast. I was also thinking that if I liked the place, I might come back and write later in the year. I wasn't sure how much I'd like the ocean in winter."

"Well, there's no snow there," Zachary said carefully.

"I actually thought that might be fun to be in a hotel and be able to write and have a hot drink while doing so. It's not like I could go anywhere then."

"So you're counting on Mother Nature to keep you at it?"

We both laughed. It was easy chatter. Zachary turned the conversation to me and my sister.

After I'd talked about how we were close, being only two years apart, with Kara being the older, I asked him about his family.

"Well, it's me now, really. My parents had wanted a big family but it just didn't happen. It's kind of a thing in my family history, having only one, sometimes two children. We have this money and this huge property but very few children."

"But you have a cousin?" I asked.

"I do. You must have met Naomi. She's probably my closest relative, having practically grown up here with me. Her mother was always in rehab. My aunt hated this place so it offered Naomi some protection from her mother's moods, which were unpredictable even when she was sober. Her father, my Uncle Darren, was a lot of help to my father, who wasn't a very good manager, at least not of the estate. I think it would have been so much more had my uncle inherited instead of my father."

I nodded, surprised at Zachary's description of his father. I had had a whole different image of him. Someone more like Richard, I guess.

"It must be nice having a cousin then, who seems close to your age, seeing as you were an only."

"Naomi and I get along okay, I guess. She doesn't like what I've done with the place. She'd have rather let Kernroote molder out here all on its own, perhaps with just us. She's like my father that way, while I resemble her father in my dreams, I guess."

I nodded, thinking about it. "I'm sure Richard and his family would have kept you from letting the castle decline too far into the dust."

Zachary gave me a look and a smile. I stepped over a long tree root that threatened to trip me. He kept pace. We were silent for a bit. I wanted to ask more about Naomi but wasn't quite sure how to.

Once again Zachary appeared to read my mind. "It's probably not true that Naomi would never have let people in. She's in IT and into all the gaming and stuff. She'd probably have set the castle up as some sort of living role playing game board complete with actors as monsters that needed to be 'killed.' She even suggested the idea to me one night when we were drinking."

The trail curved around to the left and we followed it, heading down into one of the low dips. The trees smelled good here.

"It's not something I know enough about. I figured the hotel would bring in more people. I think she hopes to see me fail. It would prove that she should have inherited instead of me," Zachary said. There was a trace of bitterness.

"But if it was your father's choice, why would he have picked Naomi?" I asked. That seemed curious.

Zachary shrugged. "In our family, sometimes a cousin inherits. It's a strange sort of family tree if you look back at owners of Kernroote. The most constant thing about it is the fact that the Perlettes—Richard's family—have always been there."

"That's different," I said. I filed away the potential conflict with Naomi. It didn't tell me why she was there though. "Does Naomi come and visit a lot now? To check, you know, to see if you've failed yet?" I laughed a little as I said that, hoping to keep Zachary at ease.

Fortunately he also smiled and chuckled a little at my commentary. "She doesn't show up much, maybe once a year or so. Sometimes I think she just gets bored every now and then and shows up to make some mischief."

We came around through the trees and they began to open up onto the back terrace of the castle.

"It really is a nice walk through there," I said.

"We can always go through the garden," Zachary said.

"I think I'd like to walk along beside it. Get a feel for how large it is," I said. "It feels so overwhelming inside but it's not what I see from the window at all."

It seemed as if Zachary's smile was a little tight, not quite natural, as if he wasn't pleased by my answer. But perhaps he had hoped to extend our conversation. Maybe he just wasn't good at covering up his emotions and he was hoping that we could get closer.

"It's been such an enjoyable talk. I hope we can do something again," I said, trying to ease that discomfort.

"I'm sure we'll be able to," Zachary said. "I could have someone bring in some lunch tomorrow. We could eat in the breakfast room if you'd like?"

"That would be lovely," I said. I realized I would have liked to see where Zachary lived in the castle, but if he wasn't willing to be forthcoming, I wasn't going to press him on it.

We finished our walk around the garden with idle chitchat that seemed loud in the silence. The birds had gone silent again and so had the cicadas. It was almost as if the proximity to the castle made creatures quiet down, afraid to be noticed. Even our feet against the gravel didn't have the sharpness of sound that they had had in the front of the place.

We made it to the door and Zachary held it open for me. I hadn't felt warm outside but it was pleasantly cool in the lobby. I could have wished for a lemonade but I doubted that would be forthcoming. Later I would have lunch. Tomorrow I would stay in here and have lunch with Zachary.

We finalized our lunch plans. Zachary was once again his charming self, even moving in towards a possible kiss when Richard came out from behind the desk and interrupted with questions about an account he needed Zachary's help with. There was an accusation in his voice that suggested Zachary should never have gone out.

I waved a helpless sort of goodbye and headed back up to my room.

Chapter 19

I opened the door to my room and found, not the luxury suite I'd been placed in, but a forest. Not the forest that I'd walked through with Zachary, which was a tame, modern forest. This one looked like a primeval forest with ferns as tall as my head and trees that grew so high I couldn't see the tops. They were contained in part by my room but the trunks appeared to go right through the floor. I wondered if I went upstairs to the third floor if that room, too, had a tree trunk. And downstairs would there be more fern?

I didn't walk in, but stood there dumbly for a few minutes. Nothing changed. I heard something groan in the room. I wasn't sure what it was.

If I was hallucinating, this was the most realistic yet. I backed away from the door. Finally I closed it and went for a walk through the second-floor wing. What I had seen was too bizarre for words and I didn't know what I'd tell Zachary if I went rushing back downstairs. I was nearly to the end of the hallway when I saw Cam returning from somewhere.

"Morning, Ms. Winter," he said.

"Morning, Cam."

"I thought your new room was over that way?" He pointed.

"Just stretching my legs some more." Why did he care?

"There's not much down here yet. I mean, the rooms are ready but we haven't used them. And they don't have balconies like yours. If you needed ice or something, I didn't want you wandering around and not being able to find it. Sometimes this place can feel like Hogwarts with things changing and doors not going where they're supposed to."

All said with a smile and charm, as if he knew what I was going through but wasn't going to refer to it.

"I can't imagine growing up here," I said, turning to walk with him. "I mean, sometimes I think if it was just you and your family and Zachary's family, it could have given you nightmares."

"I learned to talk to the house real young. You'll find if you say nice things, you never get nightmares. Or that's what my dad told me when I was real little, so that's what I've always done. It seems to work for me. Probably just the power of suggestion, huh?" There was that shy, boyish smiled.

"Probably," I said. "But maybe I'll try it if the lights go out on me again. That did kind of scare me."

"Should have called down and let us know. My dad is gruff and all but he cares about the people here, probably more than anyone."

Cam waited to watch me go into my room. I was afraid for an instant that the primeval forest would still be there, but my hallucinations appeared to be shy. They only showed up when no one else was around. The room was ordinary once again.

I went in and turned and waved, but Cam had already disappeared around the corner. I closed the door. It was only then that I worried about what would happen if I had one of those hallucinations while I was in the room. Still, it seemed better to be on the second floor than up on the fifth. I wasn't so isolated here. If I screamed loud enough there was a chance someone would hear me.

I looked in the closet and around the room to make sure there wasn't anything or anyone hiding there. Then I opened my computer. I spent some time playing on social media, wasting what was left of the morning. Then I forced myself to open my document where I'd been writing. I tensed my shoulders against the words that I'd seen there the day before.

I read the last paragraph and it was filled only with the words I'd written. There were no death threats. I breathed out. Whatever was going on, I was really losing it.

I sat in front of the computer for some time staring at the glowing screen. I read the words a hundred times and then re-read them. I started to read the last few paragraphs of my story but I hated it. It felt so light and inane. Who would want to read that?

I closed the program and got up to pace around. Everything I thought I knew or believed was being brought into question. Was I able to write? I'd always been the one to write reports for the division because I was good at that. I liked writing letters. I'd blogged here and there and people had been very responsive to my words, but I couldn't seem to write a darned book.

I settled in and opened up the browser. This time I'd share on a blog. I started up a free one and titled it "Adventures in a Modern Castle," and started writing about my impressions of the castle. I avoided using the name just in case Richard or someone monitored the Internet for mentions of the place. I didn't need him knowing I was quietly going crazy.

I wrote several posts about each day and each incident. Then I set the computer aside. I wrote nothing about Zachary. The sun was sliding down low but there wasn't yet any pink in the sky. I went out on the balcony. It was comfortably warm and there was still a breeze, which kept it from feeling too humid.

I smelled lilies and pine and earth. There were birds singing. I turned my face upwards and let the air blow on it. I felt freer than I had in a while. I needed to tell my story. I had been trapped in my mind wondering what was going on. No one was likely read my blog except Kara, but I could always tell her I was trying out something new. If someone else did read it, they wouldn't know if it were truth or fiction and I had no identifying information on my profile.

I breathed in. My chest seemed more open. I was finally really excited to meet Zachary tomorrow, at peace with being in the castle.

I settled on the balcony and enjoyed the rest of the afternoon. I was hungry and I knew I should get up and eat but I had no desire to do so. I just wanted to rest. It was like all that purging had made me sleepy. I nodded off in my chair a few times. I hadn't slept well so perhaps that was to be expected but I was still surprised. I was not normally one to nod off.

When I woke, I was chilly and the wind was a bit stronger, leaving a sort of bite to the air. I went inside, grateful to be out of the wind. It was still cool in the room but not as cool as outside. I could probably turn off the air conditioning but I decided against that. It could warm up and get humid any time. Besides, I didn't really want to leave the door open. There wasn't a screen, which would mean any mosquitos could come in and then I'd be an itchy mess.

I combed my hair and grabbed my bag. I'd drive down to the city find something cheap to eat. I hurried downstairs and out the door. Hal was still on duty and he nodded at me when he looked up from his phone. He didn't try and hide it from me. It was probably only Zachary he was worried about.

I crunched over the gravel and noticed my car looked uneven. I circled around to see what was wrong and the front tire was completely flat. The back tire wasn't completely flat yet but it was definitely low. I was going to need to call a tow truck.

I glanced back at Hal, who was busy with his phone. I could ask him if he'd seen anyone. It wasn't likely that I'd suddenly get two flat tires. My car wasn't new, but it wasn't old, either. And I'd replaced those tires only a year ago.

I marched over to Hal. He didn't look up for a moment and when he did, it was slow and rather insolent. I wondered if he'd been the one to let the air out.

"I have two flat tires. Did you see anyone around my car?"

Hal shrugged. "We've had some guests. And I've been in and out so I couldn't say. When was the last time you were out?"

"Yesterday."

"Coulda picked up a nail. There's a lot of construction around." He looked back at his phone. No help.

I went inside and marched into lobby. Richard wasn't at the front desk but I headed there anyway. I drummed my fingers on the counter. No one. I was getting angry. I was scared, too. I admitted that. There were strange things happening and now I didn't have a way to leave even if I wanted to.

I pulled out my phone and noted the time. I gave Richard a minute to come out and see what all the drumming was about. Then I tried "Hello?" quiet at first and another time more loudly. The second call brought Naomi.

"Ms. Winter. I'm sorry. I was at the computer in back and the walls here are thick." I wondered where Richard had disappeared to.

"Yes. Two of my tires are flat. It happened while my car was in the parking lot here. I'll need someone to tow it or something so I can get new tires but I want that reported."

Naomi's eyes narrowed as she looked at me, nodding. She picked up the phone and punched a button.

"It's me. I'm at the front desk with Ms. Winter. She has two flat tires on her car."

She listened to something and nodded again. "I'll tell her."

"I called Richard. He's in the other office, downstairs. He'll call a tow for you and charge it to the hotel. Have you talked to the person on duty at the door?"

"I tried," I said. "But he wasn't very helpful."

"No doubt," Naomi said. "I'll go have a word with him. Were you out to meet friends?"

"I was just going to go find some dinner," I said.

"That I can help you with," she said. "Let me write this up before I talk to Hal. Dinner is on the house, as clearly there was a problem and our doormen weren't on duty as they should have been. If someone were vandalizing guest's cars, he should have been aware of the fact and noticed something."

"Thank you." I was grateful. I would have liked to get away from the castle, but surprisingly I wasn't as upset as I would have been the other day. At least when things happened here, they worked hard to make it right.

I went up the stairs to the dining room. I heard serving noises and a bit of conversation but it wasn't loud. I looked inside. The waiter hurried over. There was no set person just seating people. Surprisingly, there was a large group of businessmen sitting around the bar talking. Clearly the restaurant was known.

It was a bit early, even for a weekday, but there were two other tables filled, one with a couple and one with a group of six, including a teenager who looked bored. I wondered about their outing.

"Just one?"

I nodded. He took me to a booth near the window. I wasn't surprised to see Chris seated in a booth, looking at an e-reader, a glass of beer near his hand. He looked up as I was about to be seated.

"If you're alone, I've barely begun," he said. He set the reader aside and looked at me hopefully, almost like a puppy dog wishing for company.

I smiled, suddenly grateful for company. Ordinary company where I wasn't trying to find things out. He seemed comfortable around e-readers, but did that mean he could hack into a person's computer and write odd notes? It didn't seem as if it was something a guest could do.

The waiter led me there. I asked to have a glass of whatever Chris was having. It seemed like the polite thing to do. And honestly, I do like beer now and then.

"How was your day?" he asked.

"All right," I said. "You said your hobby was ghost hunting. What sorts of things have you heard about this place? Although if they're real scary, I'm not sure I want to know. I hear enough strange noises in the night." I tried to laugh as if I were just making conversation.

Chris blushed again, just a little. He shrugged. "Most of it is legend. as the place hasn't been open to the public for long. I happened to read about the opening on one of the forums I frequent and someone was talking about how this would be an awesome place to explore for ghosts because it's so old and there are so many legends."

"Like?" I prompted.

"Things like the old owners making people disappear from time to time. People in Asheville—when it was a tiny place a hundred years ago—seeing strange lights from this side of town. In the late nineteenth century, when the rich would come to the mountains to cool off, I heard that the Kernrootes tried to become part of that set, but that one of the rich young women partying here disappeared. No one found her body. The place closed for a few years and then another Kernroote was in charge and had a large soiree, as I guess they were called then, about a decade later. Guests said they heard a girl crying from somewhere in the house. A few others who stayed in the house overnight claimed that they felt as if something was watching them. One man said he was grabbed by a shadow. The rumors went on and the stories grew until the Kernrootes stopped giving parties and they were slowly erased from the social register of the area."

"And have you heard anyone crying?" I asked.

The waiter returned for my order and asked Chris if he'd like to wait for his. Chris said he would. I ordered the minestrone soup and the shrimp skewers. I wasn't particularly hungry even after my hike and both of those sounded light enough.

"I haven't heard anything," Chris said. "In fact, the

place seems mostly ordinary, if a little big and a little emptier than I'd expect. But they've just opened and not everything is done."

I nodded.

"Have you had anything weird happen?"

I considered telling him everything but I didn't want to sound too crazy. "Well, two of my tires are flat this evening, otherwise I'd have gone into town." I laughed. "I doubt that was a ghost, though. The other night in the storm, the fifth floor power went out. Richard said it was probably a fuse but there were a lot of odd noises, probably from the storm. Still, it was scary in the moment. I can imagine how the guests staying here after a party and plenty of drinking would have thought they heard or saw stuff."

Chris nodded.

Our food came. Chris had ordered a steak, which was huge. He seemed appalled by the size. My shrimp skewers were more delicate. The soup bowl was good sized and there was a large cheese platter with breads and crackers that came with it.

"I didn't order that," Chris said.

"Complimentary," the waiter said, smiling.

"Thank you," Chris and I said at about the same time.

The waiter left us to our meals. Chris took a moment to test the steak and cut into it. I noticed he liked his steaks rare. He nodded in satisfaction as the red blood flowed easily out of the slab of meat.

"This is far more than I was expecting," he said, some-what apologetically.

"It is huge. I'm glad I didn't order one."

"It's a nice enough restaurant. I can't believe there are no signs in the lobby, though," Chris said. "I had to go exploring around to find it."

I nodded, knowing what he meant.

"Have you done much of that?" he asked me. "Exploring? I want to go down to the basement and subbasement, but not sure…" He blushed a little again.

"I accidentally went down to the basement one day. There seemed to be a laundry there. It's funny, though, because the basement seemed to run under the parking area as well as the building," I said.

Chris made a hmmph sound. We continued eating. I spread a bit of thick cheese on a piece of warm bread. It was heavenly. Even the smell was enough to make me groan with pleasure.

Chris and I chatted about other things. In real life, Chris was an electrical engineer. He worked a company in the tech triangle doing whatever it was that engineers did. I wasn't that savvy. It did not seem, though, that he was the sort of person who would be able to hack a computer.

He had a brother and a sister, both married. He was divorced, although it had been a number of years for him. I opened up to him about my husband leaving me.

"He's a foolish man," Chris said, and then took a big gulp of beer and changed the subject.

I felt my cheeks turn pink but I liked it. It was a nice compliment.

When we finished eating, the waiter asked us if we'd like dessert.

We both declined.

"Then thank you for your patronage," the waiter said.

"But…" Chris started.

The waiter held up a hand. "Mr. Kernroote was quite distressed about what happened to Ms. Winter's car. She has a certificate for a free evening, which she graciously shared with you, so there's no charge tonight."

Chris and I looked at each other. "Well, thanks for dinner, then," Chris said with a laugh.

I smiled. "Perhaps you'll have to return the favor, although without the flat tires." I laughed, too.

The waiter joined us and then added, "Mr. Kernroote has even called his own mechanic and a tow truck to make sure you have your car back promptly."

"Service," Chris said.

I nodded.

Chris and I chatted pleasantly about movies and music and our favorite television series to binge watch while we finished our beers. Then we stood up to go, I found that I was reluctant to let the magic of the evening end. It had been such a normal evening, with no stress of what to say and no stress of wondering how Chris would react to things. I mean, I hadn't told him everything, but I felt so much freer with him than with Zachary.

We walked around the catwalk that would take me back to the room and Chris to the elevator, looking down over the lobby. The desk was empty but there were a couple looking at the pictures on the wall down below. They were one of the couples that had been in the restaurant.

"I don't know how people can stay here. It's always so cold, even with the new decorations." I heard the woman whisper, which carried up to where I was walking so clearly she might have been standing beside me.

The husband shushed her. "We've lived here forever so we know more. The people here, they come for a night or two. Nothing will happen to them."

"I wish the restaurant had an outside entrance so we didn't have to walk through here. I feel as if there's something grabbing on to me." There was almost a note of hysteria in her voice. I found it interesting that she didn't feel that in the restaurant.

"It's clearly time to get home," the husband said, taking her hand and guiding her out.

"It's probably because Richard isn't here. He always makes things better."

"Shhh."

The door opened and they were outside. I had half a mind to go running after them. So they found Richard as someone who made things better. Certainly my experiences of him were quite different.

Chris and I gave each other a look. "Apparently there are still rumors," Chris said. We reached the elevators and he stopped, punching the down button. He must be on the first floor.

"Clearly," I replied.

"Do you need me to walk you to your room? I'd hate for you to be snatched by those ghost arms."

I smiled. "I think I'm good. It was a lovely evening."

Chris brightened, as if surprised. "It was, wasn't it?"

The elevator came then and he slowly got in while I walked around the corner to my room.

It was felt pretty silent on this side of the second floor. I almost wished I were closer to the restaurant, where there were noises and people coming and going and things there seemed more normal than things in the rest of this place. It was as if the sheer numbers of outsiders made that part of the castle normal instead of shadowy and strange. What had that couple meant? Why would they brave the restaurant if they thought there was something to fear?

I got to the room door and I hesitated. After the last time, I was more than a little worried about opening the door. My heart pounded as I inserted the key. I had to try it twice, as the first time I hesitated, pulling the key out for too long and the lock didn't unlatch. The second time it worked and I slowly opened the door.

Fearfully I peeked inside, but there was only a hotel room, larger than most, quieter than normal, but still the one I was using. There were no primeval forests, no shadows or ghosts or anything else out of the ordinary. I let out a breath and walked inside.

Chapter 20

I spent the rest of the evening working on the computer and watching television. I considered writing up the conversation I'd overheard for my blog, but it didn't quite feel right. Saying "engineering" almost felt too identifiable, which was strange. For some reason it seemed important that I make both the place and myself anonymous.

A bit later, I snuggled into bed, enjoying the comfort of the mattress and the fresh smell of the sheets. I even slept through the night with no horrible dreams. I had one strange one where Chris and Zachary were fighting over me, a duel complete with guns. Then the guns got lost and they couldn't decide what to do next. It made me smile to think of it and made me worry about my sanity that I thought two men were fighting over me.

I got up in the morning and made my way downstairs. I had breakfast at my usual table, back to the eggs this time, a nice eggs Benedict. Not as perfect as their other meals but quite good nonetheless. The waitress was polite though she seemed disinclined to chat with me, no matter that we'd spent several mornings together.

There was an older man, distinguished with hair graying at his temples, sitting alone at another table. I wondered if he too was a guest. Chris was nowhere around and I wondered if he was off hiking again, or perhaps exploring the basement, looking for ghosts. If I were ghost hunting, I'd probably explore in the daylight first, but that was just me and perhaps why I wasn't even a hobby ghost hunter.

I finished eating and left the breakfast room without seeing anyone I knew. No appearance by Zachary, no Chris, not even Naomi put in an appearance gliding by a window off on an errand known only to her.

Back in my room, I made some more coffee in the coffeepot thoughtfully provided in the sitting area and sat outside on the balcony to watch the world while I waited to go meet Zachary for lunch. I wondered when my car would be done. It had been late last night so chances were they'd do the tires later this morning. Hopefully I'd have my car by evening.

I looked up and noticed that the clouds had gotten thick and gray. It was cooler than yesterday but certainly not cold. The wind whipped around more, not a gentle breeze any longer but the sort of wind that you get when a storm is coming in. We were probably in for a thunderstorm in the afternoon.

Normally I liked storms and I liked being able to watch the thunder and lightning from inside my home, but I wasn't eager to face another storm while staying at Kernroote. The last one had been noisier than I needed and it wasn't even the thunder that was troubling. It was the castle. As if the storm energies riled it up or something.

The skunk smell came back on one of the gusts of wind, causing my nose to wrinkle. It seemed to want to hang around so I went inside to get away from it. I closed the door quickly to make sure that the scent didn't get inside.

I went over the sitting area to try and work on my book. The television blinked on. I hadn't turned it on. I searched around for the remote to turn it off, noting as I did so that the program seemed to be an ordinary talk show and not some odd horror movie about things I had seen down in the basement of the castle.

Finding the remote, I turned the television off, which left the room in silence. I might not have wanted to listen to the TV, but the silence left in the wake of turning it off felt oppressive. It was the calm before the storm that was most certainly coming.

The hairs on the back of my neck stood up. I turned slowly towards the window but there was nothing there. I began to search the room, making sure I really was alone in the suite.

The bathroom and closet were exactly as I had left them. I heard nothing at all. It was so quiet I almost worried I had lost my hearing. There was a part of me that wanted to turn the television back on just to hear something, anything. I grabbed my key and went out into the hallway. Still silent.

I walked silently across the carpet and around the catwalk. Closer to the restaurant, although it was still too early for it to be open, I heard the clatter of forks and knives and the faintest strains of music. I almost begged to go in there to join the people working merely for the companionship and the ordinary conversation. Instead, I turned to go back to my room.

It still wasn't time to meet Zachary.

Once back inside my suite, it was quiet but not threatening like it had been a few moments ago. I shook my head. It was such a little thing. Was it worth writing down?

I considered doing so, but when the television turned on again the thought tumbled out of my mind.

This time it wasn't a talk show. This time it was just the old-time snow and the fuzz of a channel that wasn't in focus. I thought I heard words here and there but couldn't make them out. I walked closer to the sitting room television. I saw shadows moving around but there was still too much fuzz to make anything out. I located the remote with ease and I turned the television back off. I sighed.

I settled onto the sofa and put my feet up. I held the remote in case the TV decided to turn itself back on again. I wondered if the strange goings-on were part of the coming storm. At least this was more playful than threatening.

On the fifth floor I had felt stalked. Here I felt like something was playing with me, although I couldn't be certain what.

I pulled out my computer. Time to write a little more on my adventures. I could add in the couple's conversation, without using names, and I could also write about the television that liked me to watch it. I had no comments on any of the posts, which meant that Kara probably thought this was all fiction. It was just as well.

By the time I had finished, it was nearly time to meet Zachary.

I went into the bathroom and freshened up a bit. My outfit didn't look wrinkled and I had no crumbs to brush off the navy blue top I had on. The white capris remained spotless, though this was the second time I had worn them. I was going to have to send out for laundry soon.

I ran a comb through my hair, checked my makeup, and satisfied myself that I was presentable before I left the room.

It was quiet in the hotel as I walked around the catwalk

but it wasn't silent. I heard male voices, one probably Zachary's and one probably Richard's, but I couldn't be certain. I made my way slowly around the catwalk, hoping they would be in a place where I could listen in but from the way they were muffled, I suspected they were in the breakfast room. It was too bad the door wasn't open so I could hear more.

But when nothing was forthcoming no matter how hard I listened, I continued on around and went down the stairs to the lobby area. As I had surmised, Richard was in the breakfast room with Zachary. The girl who worked as a waitress in the morning was there too. She was pouring water into glasses, ignoring the men who were talking on the far side of the room.

I hesitated going in, noticing their body language. Zachary's arms were crossed whereas Richard was reaching out towards his employer. Clearly whatever Zachary had decided, Richard was hoping to change his mind—at least that was how I read the language. But with Zachary one never knew.

I took a breath and pulled at the door to go in. It opened easily and without a sound, but when I had stepped in the room and looked around, both men were silent and staring at me. So was the girl.

"Am I early?" I asked. I had thought I was right on time.

"No. Not at all!" Zachary said, coming over to me. "We're just about set and Richard was going over some last-minute business. Unfortunately, we also have some bad news about your car. The tires that it needs aren't in stock locally so they had to send to Charlotte, which means it won't be ready until tomorrow."

"Really?" I said. I couldn't believe my car tires were that unusual. You'd think that the dealer would at least have them and I suspected that Asheville had at least one of every car dealer around. I didn't want to look too skeptical so I said nothing more, waiting to see what else would be offered.

Richard just nodded his head and went to brush by me. I watched him go and when he looked up enough to see me watching, his eyes met mine with what I thought was a rather defiant look.

Zachary gestured at the table, which was set for two. It wasn't my usual table, which was further down. This one was closer to the door that led outside but as the room wasn't open to the general public, chances were no one would be coming inside. The waitress closed the blinds to the main room but left the ones to the outside open.

"We'll be having tomato basil soup, a specialty bread that I've had made for today, and croissants with bacon, lettuce, tomato, and avocado. I hope that's to your liking?"

"It sounds wonderful," I said.

"Good." Zachary nodded. "I have lemonade or we have sweet tea in the kitchen. If you prefer wine we can open a bottle from upstairs."

"No, lemonade will be fine. It's a bit early for wine."

"I had a feeling that lunch was a little too early for a cocktail, particularly if you plan to go back upstairs to work."

I laughed a little. "I seem to have gotten to a stuck point so I have no idea if I'll be working later on today."

"Well, I can't advise going for a walk. There's a storm blowing in from the west. It's supposed to be quite a big one," Zachary said. "I'm glad you're no longer on the upper floor. I suspect it would be far too noisy to get any sort of rest."

"Last time I did manage to fall asleep eventually. Fortunately most storms don't last that long."

"The first of three," Zachary said. "The weather the last few days has been warm enough that they expect quite a lot of thunder and lightning. You might be trapped here longer than just today if there are many downed trees. They won't be able to get your car back to the hotel and no one could drive you out."

It bothered me that he was talking about how I'd be trapped there, as if I needed a way out. He couldn't know how unnerved the place made me, could he? Or maybe he just wanted reassurance that I loved staying there, but that wasn't something I was willing to give, not just then.

We made small talk over the soup. Zachary talked more about his childhood and growing up in his strange family while we ate. It was more than small talk and felt genuine. When he looked at me, he often shook his head. "I sound like I'm whining," he said finally, after talking about how kids were always afraid of his home and he had the reputation of being weird because of it.

"Not at all. Just a true memory," I said. "And kids can be cruel when anyone is a little different."

Zachary gave me a genuine smile that time that seemed to light up his face. "I always wanted someone who could understand that. I have to admit I used to dream of having the power to show them, you know? I guess money is power, but I know there are a few who have stayed around and are hoping the hotel fails."

"Now that's horrible. And it's on them," I said. "You've worked hard at this." I didn't say that it was a creepy place and I didn't ask why he hadn't promoted it more so that there were more people around. It wasn't my business. At best, we might have a fling, but I couldn't see myself staying in the castle. It wasn't in me.

Zachary began by asking me about my younger years and who I wished I could show off success to. I had to laugh because clearly that person would be Daniel. I couldn't tell Zachary that I needed to know I was desirable again. When we had finished our croissant sandwiches, he scooted his chair closer to mine so that his knees were pressing against mine, pushing my legs apart.

He asked me more about my writing. Then he surprised me by talking about one of my favorite Nora Roberts books. The shock must have shown on my face.

"I don't normally tell people that," he said. "Honestly, I was surprised I liked it, but I was trying to impress a girl a long time ago and she loved Nora Roberts."

I laughed. It was such a sweet thing to do.

There was a slight gap in one of the blinds and I saw Chris walk through the main area. He paused, looking more closely at the room, clearly aware that the blinds weren't normally pulled. I wondered how much darker it made the lobby, considering how much of the light came through the large back windows. I think he glimpsed Zachary because he was about to continue through, but then he caught my eye.

His face fell slightly but then he turned away. That slight blush that had to be the bane of his fair-haired existence rushed to his face, and he hurried through the side door and out to the stairs that would take him around the garden.

I felt badly, having a sudden urge to run out and talk to him, to tell him that Zachary was handsome, yes, attractive, yes, but really nothing serious. But that assumed a level of interest on his part that I wasn't completely certain of. For all I knew, he was would rather spend time with Zachary than me, although I didn't really believe that, deep down.

"It really is too bad about your car," Zachary said, turning the conversation back. "I hate that such a thing

could happen here. Richard talked to the tow truck oper-
ator and it did look like someone had purposefully
damaged them. We have so few guests, I'd hate to think
that one of them would do such a thing."

"Things happen and you certainly can't control who
you offer rooms to," I said, conciliatory, wondering if
Zachary had caught Chris's look and was worried there
was something between us.

"It's the least we can do," Zachary said. "And I'm
pleased that you aren't running away or writing horrible
reviews on the hotel sites. I'm finally approved for a couple
of them and am starting to get some bookings."

"I bet that feels good."

"I'm hopeful that by spring I'll have a full house—or
perhaps castle is a better term?"

"That soon?" I was surprised at how quickly he
expected things to pick up.

"I should have the rest of the rooms done by then and
our reservations are up. I plan to have a gala for the grand
opening of when everything is completed, rather than the
soft opening I've had going on now. I figure this way staff is
getting used to what is expected of them and working at
the castle. Word of mouth will mean that the paid advertising I do for the gala will go further."

I smiled and nodded. It was a sound plan. Not that I'd
be coming back for a grand opening or telling anyone to
go, not unless they wanted to have a really creepy
experience.

At that moment Zachary's hand dropped to my knee,
sending a shocked thrill through my body. A deep, aching
longing followed. Something must have shown on my face
because he removed his hand just as quickly as he'd placed
it there.

"I should let you get back to your ruminations. That's what writers do when they're stuck, isn't it?" he asked.

I was disappointed that he was ending our lunch. I wondered if it was because he'd let himself be too familiar and I hadn't reacted the way he thought. There seemed to be a great deal of shyness about this man.

"It can always wait, but I'm sure you have other work to be done here," I said.

Zachary just gave me a look that suggested he was regretting sending me away. We both rose at the same time and he courteously escorted me to my room. This time when I opened the door, the room looked ordinary enough. I turned back to thank him for lunch but he was there behind me, so close that I practically walked into him. Our noses knocked and he gave me a chaste kiss and started to draw back. By this time, my arms were around his neck and I pulled him to me, giving him a decidedly not very chaste kiss that lasted much longer than I expected.

For once I was glad of how quiet the hotel was. I didn't think anything more about it as Zachary quietly closed the door after we'd somehow ended up in my room.

Chapter 21

After an afternoon of dozing, I woke up when Zachary was getting up and dressing.

"Work awaits," he said softly.

I smiled back at him, enjoying looking at his body. That ache that had been building was finally satisfied. I was satisfied. I stretched, thinking I should get up and change. I hadn't heard anything about my car, but I could go down to the desk and find out. No doubt if anything had changed, Richard would know.

After Zachary left, I got up and showered, changed, and looked at my computer. I considered whether I should post something about the afternoon but decided that was too intimate. Perhaps fodder for later romance writing, but not for the blog, which was more about the strange stuff going on.

I considered trying to write but couldn't force myself to open the document. I didn't want to see something negative there. I also didn't feel like going back and reading it again to get myself into the mood. I hadn't liked it the last time I'd started reading. What if I hated it again? Did I have what took to start over from scratch?

I lurked online and read some things in social media. The sun was sliding beyond the horizon and I suspected I'd need food soon enough. I hadn't gotten another gift certificate but it wasn't as if I couldn't afford the meals in the restaurant. I had snacks here and I could even do a light dinner.

I wondered if I went to the restaurant whether I'd run into Chris again. Of course if I did and he ignored me, I didn't think I could take that. I decided to eat in.

The wind rattled the glass, startling me after the silence of the day. Hail began to fall, pelting the glass and the sides of the building. I got up to look out. The hail wasn't large but there was a lot of it.

Thunder rolled through and lightning cracked, almost on top of the thunder. The storm was clearly just overhead and it had come in quickly. With any luck it would leave just as quickly.

Instead the hail picked up even more, coming down so fast that it was hard to see. I felt sorry for any birds or other small creatures who happened to be caught out in this. I backed away from the window.

I cracked open the sliding door to check out the storm. It wasn't facing the angle of the wind, so I was still somewhat protected while watching the hail. It smelled like rain and a little like something burning. Lightning cracked in the sky once more, coming so low it appeared to hit the ground. Perhaps I was smelling the beginnings of a fire.

The hail turned to rain but continued to fall in sheets without stop. A clap of thunder hit right overhead and I jumped.

Lightning flashed.

The lights snapped off.

As I was in the doorway, watching the storm, I saw that the lights around the courtyard, set discretely outside the first floor rooms, all snapped off. The faint glow from my right that was no doubt the restaurant also disappeared. The sun hadn't quite gone down but the world was left in shades of gray.

I closed the door and went to find the flashlight I'd purchased. One greenish light now glowed in the room. It was clearly an emergency light. I found it interesting that there weren't emergency lights on the fifth floor. I could have used them the other night when I'd been feeling around in the dark for batteries.

I wondered about going out to the restaurant. There would be other people around and no doubt the loss of power would make for great conversation.

Then I wondered what Zachary was doing. Was he doing what he could to make sure the patrons of the restaurant felt okay about their dinners?

I jumped when I heard a knock at the door. But then perhaps it was Zachary coming to rescue me from the storm. I turned and hurried over, still carrying my flashlight.

I opened the door and it was indeed Zachary. I felt a flutter of excitement in my belly, like a schoolgirl who gets to see her crush.

"I was worried that you'd find this too noisy and frightening, especially after your ordeal on the fifth floor," he said.

He wasn't smiling. Instead there was a look of intense concern.

"I've been doing okay here," I said. "But I wouldn't mind company."

"Actually, I can't stay. I have to go check on the emergency power. Do you want to come?"

I hesitated.

He smiled. "I'm not sure I want to go running around down in the basement, really, but I don't know where Richard has gone."

I nodded and grabbed my room key. I left my flashlight in the room. It was probably not the smartest move ever but by the time I realized I had done it, it was far too late.

Zachary led me down the hall away from the main lobby stairs and the elevator. At the end of the hallway, where the hall made a right turn, there was an ell with a door. That door was another fire stair.

The stairwell had only one green emergency light above the door. The rest of the stairs were shrouded in darkness. I saw the glow from the light above the first floor but I'd have to walk down the stairs by feel. Zachary pulled out a small pen light that offered enough glow to make hurrying downstairs safer.

I followed him, staying close. "Does this happen often?"

"Not really. We lose power about a third of the time when storms blow through but usually it's just a flicker. We have a backup generator for the emergency lights. Normally that works the kitchen as well but for some reason that's out tonight. Unfortunately, I can't find Richard to go take care of it," Zachary said.

"Is he the one who usually fixes it?"

"He or Cam. Cam's not really employed here officially. He helps out because he helps his dad, kind of like helping out around the house, but I can't order him to do things. They aren't indentured servants or anything. They work here by choice."

I nodded, though he was ahead of me on the stairs and it was doubtful he could see my agreement.

We passed the door to the first floor and the soft green

light. As we headed deeper down towards the basement I noticed there wasn't another light on. Clearly there were no emergency lights for the employees, which seemed a rather unsafe thing. What if Zachary had to send someone besides Richard or Cam down here? I had no doubt Richard and Cam knew the castle as well as anyone, but a worker wouldn't necessarily know it.

A bang made me jump. It even made Zachary pause. In the dim light, I saw him frown. We both stood for a moment on the stairs, waiting, but saw nothing.

Zachary turned back and kept going downwards. We passed a door that I thought went to the basement.

"Shouldn't we have gone in there?" I asked when he kept going.

"The generators are on the lowest level. It was easiest to vent them there." He said.

I remembered seeing the furnace in the basement, that large body of a thing that seemed to take up a huge amount of space under the one wing. And then there'd been the strange square thing that I had taken for a generator, but what did I know?

I felt the faintest trickle of unease seep through my body. Was it safe to be there with Zachary? Maybe I should have stayed in my room.

"I should have said that I'm kind of afraid of going into caves and stuff," I started.

Zachary laughed. "You can go back up if you want."

I turned, thinking I'd just follow the stairwell upwards, but the lack of a green light on the basement door meant it was too dark for me to do that safely. "I didn't bring my flashlight," I said. "I guess you're stuck with me."

"There are worse things," he said, giving me a look and a half smile.

I smiled back. I hoped that in the dim light even

Zachary wouldn't notice that it wasn't my real smile. I didn't like this at all. I was following this guy down into the depths of the basement.

Of course, really, did I have to worry? My sister knew I was staying there. What kind of hotel kills all their customers?

Naturally I thought about my tires being slashed.

Naturally I thought about horror movies where the heroine goes blindly to her death.

What if this was the sort of thing Zachary did? He brought people here—lured them, as it were—and then killed them in a sub-basement. Then again, maybe he was in it with Richard. My imagination was definitely going overtime and likely I'd have at least one nice long post for the blog I'd started about my adventures.

We reached the bottom of the stairs. Zachary opened the heavy door and then we were in a large room. Next to the door was a silver metal box with dials on it. I was reminded of the machines in old horror movies. Great, now I was thinking I was in a B movie from the 1950s. And me without a flashlight.

Another crash. I thought I saw the flicker of a light upstairs, which chilled me even more. What if the lights were already coming on?

"This is the main generator," Zachary said, drawing my attention. "There's a smaller one for upstairs but that just runs my quarters and Richard's home on the seventh floor."

So I had seen a generator up there.

"There's a bunch of electrical stuff up there too. It's not as easy as just plugging the thing in, although it's set to transfer power over if it needs to be done. It was a huge expense for the hotel. This thing is heavy and you can't believe what a pain it was to get it down here." Zachary handed me the penlight while he looked at some of the dials. I had no idea what I was seeing.

He opened something on the side that looked to me a bit like a fuse panel and started flipping some buttons. A second later a few old naked bulbs came on overhead.

"Yes!" he said, using a fist pump. "We're in business."

In the full light, the room wasn't any more inviting. It was an old cellar type of sub-basement. There was cement here, leveling the generator, but the rest of the floor was earth. The walls were brick near the generator but the rest were stone and I mean set stone like they used before you had mortar. This place really was ancient.

I wandered over to the far wall where there was stone. "This place is ancient, isn't it?"

"It is," Zachary said. "Want to see one of my favorite areas? It's down a corridor and is kind of creepy but hopefully the generator will keep working and we won't end up walking in the dark."

"That would so not be fun," I admitted. "Is it safe?"

"I've lived here all my life and nothing has ever killed me. It's just creepy. Like it's the heart of the place."

I looked into the other room even as a chill ran down my back. He'd called the pond the heart of the place too. Another thump as if someone was trying to open the door behind us but not succeeding. Zachary looked over at the large door he'd let shut and frowned. Maybe it was best I follow him.

Zachary gestured for me to follow him through to the next room. It was another large open basement room lined with stone, so far as I could see in from the light that leaked in through from the room behind me. There were lanterns along the walls, and one bare bulb in the center of the room, the wiring obvious. Boxes littered the room, placed for a moment that had stretched into years.

At the far side of the large room, I noticed an old furnace, the huge old kind that required coal to be shoveled in. It was dark and cool now, but it must have gotten really hot in here when it was in use.

"Our old ancient furnace," Zachary said, nodding at me. "I used to think it was the creepiest thing here when I was a kid. I hadn't found the other room yet. I worried that someone would take me down here and feed me to it when it was burning. I didn't know that it hadn't been used in years and that I wasn't likely to end up in there getting burned to death."

I nodded, thinking how he had picked up my thoughts. We could be good together in some ways. We were very good together physically and clearly we were both imaginative. I shouldn't have been surprised that he was imaginative given his ideas about the castle and the hotel. It was too bad he could be so cold and unfeeling at times.

We passed through another doorframe. This one was also large but it was piled with old furniture or at least old furniture frames. There were no cushions of any sort but there were old bedframes and at least two old dressers minus the drawers. There were shelving units along the walls and they were piled with toys that had seen better days. I wasn't sure if any of the toys were modern. They were all things I had seen in magazines and pictures but had never had of my own.

This was all lit by two more bare bulbs. Zachary found an electric lantern by the door, a modern anachronism that suggested that someone visited the subbasement with some regularity. He turned it on and picked it up, holding it before him.

"I have no idea why they kept all these old bed frames. My grandfather or someone must have cleared out all the beds at one time and placed the frames here. If we had mattresses with them, someone at least got rid of those."

"What about the drawers in the dresser?" I asked.

Zachary rolled his eyes and shrugged. "Who knows? Maybe if we'd kept them they'd have been something I could sell as antiques or used in certain rooms, but these are just old and quite damaged."

We passed through another room that held boxes and bags. A dressmaker's dummy was in the corner and I jumped a little as we passed it. There was an old bicycle down here, one with the large front wheel. Again something out of a picture book but not real life.

"We've never gone through the boxes. Richard says it's mostly clothing and has cleared out a bit of it. If I hadn't remodeled and made this a hotel, no doubt he'd spend all his time here clearing away this clutter. He hates clutter," Zachary said. "It probably drives him nuts knowing it's here. If Cam goes to work for me after he graduates, he'll probably get to man the upstairs and Richard will spend hours down here clearing out."

I was curious about the boxes myself. If they belonged to my family, I'd want to know more. I was surprised that Zachary could just pass these by without much curiosity. But then, as a child, he'd probably satisfied himself that the boxes held nothing of interest and didn't worry about it again.

We must have been under the main lobby area when Zachary made a turn. Instead of heading towards the far door that no doubt led to another room packed with stuff, he went in a different direction passing, through an aisle of wood furniture, some items clearly broken. On top of an old wooden desk, a stuffed raccoon glared at us. It was poorly enough done that I wasn't fooled into believing it was real even for a moment.

Zachary picked his way through a path known only to him. An old wooden armoire, reaching nearly six feet high with all the carvings on the top, practically blocked the path that he was making but Zachary just stepped around it. I followed behind him, and was surprised to see a closed wooden door, reinforced with metal bands just beyond. That path was more clearly open with just some more trunks and a few odd dolls settled on top of them.

There seemed to be too much stuff for one family, but then again they'd been in the place for hundreds of years. Longer if the legends were true. Plus it wouldn't be just their things. Likely some of this had belonged to Richard's family as well.

"Told you it got creepy," Zachary said, watching me eye the doorway. "If you want to stop now, we can."

"I'm fine," I said.

"I know you don't like caves and this gets cave-like down here. There are a few lights, but…"

I shrugged.

Zachary opened the door. There were lanterns, old kerosene lanterns burning along the corridor. I wondered if they burned all the time. We weren't in a room, we were in a corridor. It was longer than I expected. It probably went all the way out to the courtyard garden, which made me shiver.

"We aren't under the house anymore, are we?" I asked.

"I think here we are," Zachary said. "I'm not sure when we stop being under the house and start being under the courtyard. This corridor actually has another exit in the woods. There aren't really any trails up there but if we were ever attacked, you could run through here and out into the woods."

"Well, that's good to know if we have peasants with torches coming after us."

That made him laugh. It wasn't an unpleasant laugh but the acoustics in the corridor were unfortunate, making him sound like a maniac. Here and there the walls were shorn up with beams of old wood as if we were in a mine rather than in a sub-basement. In one spot there was a pile of rocks, as if there'd been a cave-in, which creeped me out. Zachary didn't seem to notice it, suggesting he was far too familiar with the corridor.

I considered going back, even paused behind Zachary, but I heard the echo of something fall behind us. If there was someone else down there, I didn't exactly want to be alone. I tried to tell myself it was likely only Richard, but the look on Zachary's face when he turned to see made me reconsider. He looked a bit worried.

I wanted to say something but couldn't make the words come out. Instead I hurried along towards him and he turned to continue our trek.

I regretted my decision to follow and wondered if I could persuade Zachary to take me back upstairs, but just then he stopped at a door. This one was also old and wooden but it wasn't latched. Zachary looked at the latch, frowning.

Before he could say anything, the door swung open slowly. It had the slightest creak that echoed through the hallway and then stopped like it was cut off, dead. I swallowed, feeling my heart rate accelerate. Now I was really regretting this.

Richard stepped out of the doorway. "Zachary," he said, looking at Zachary. Then he looked over at me. His eyes widened and his mouth gaped open just a little.

"Ms. Winter. This is no place for you. You'll want to return to the lobby at once."

I stepped back, not so much at his order and the

thought of following it, but the way he said it. It was beyond strange.

"She's here with me. She *agreed* to come." Zachary put the emphasis strongly on the word *agreed* as if that made all the difference.

There was the slightest tremble and the lanterns began to flicker, like a fire about to go out. I pulled back even further, wondering what was happening. Shadows started to dance in the corridor.

Richard narrowed his eyes at me. "Let's go." He stepped around Zachary and took my arm. His hand pressed into my upper arm with such force that I gasped.

"Let her go," Zachary said. "You're hurting her."

Richard said nothing, just marching out of the corridor. I tried to pull my arm away from him.

"I can follow you if you let go of my arm," I hissed. I wasn't sure I wanted to. There was something grim in his manner.

"Let her go," Zachary called. I heard him moving behind us, running towards Richard. I pulled at the man and our progress halted.

"If you know what's good for you, you'll get out of here," Richard said. "And out of the hotel. Tonight. Cam can drive you."

Zachary reached us, his hand grabbing Richard's arm, pulling it away from mine.

My arm was released suddenly. I stood there rubbing it, wondering what Richard meant. I didn't like this. I didn't intend to stay around in the sub-basement with two men who could easily be mad. I hurried along the corridor. The lights flickered overhead as I passed them.

Large, shadowed hands reached out towards me but the shadows stayed on the walls. A tree root broke through the ground beneath my feet, startling me. I jumped back, practically falling.

"Stop it," Richard hissed.

I didn't turn. Didn't know what he was talking about. I didn't like him, wasn't sure I trusted him, but I didn't like the downstairs area at all.

The door we had entered the corridor through banged against the wall and then slammed shut. I jumped again. I ran towards it but as I expected, it wouldn't budge for me. I looked around. I didn't see Richard. It was like my nightmare.

"Come on," Zachary said, hurrying towards me. "We can go the other way. He won't know the forest, especially not in the storm." He pulled me, gently, and we ran towards the far end, the one that he had promised went out to the forest. Zachary paused again near the room Richard had come out of. The door was closed once more.

I heard the door at the end of the corridor bang again.

"I bet we can hide," Zachary said, pulling open the door.

I worried Richard might have gone inside. He wasn't in the corridor any longer.

I worried about trying to hide. In movies, when you hide, they always find you.

But Zachary had pulled me inside before I voiced any of my worries.

There were no lights in here but there was a glow, a faint green glow that was different from the emergency lights over the doors. This was softer and it swirled. In front of me the floor was only partly dirt and partly the roots of a huge tree. The roots were so wide that if they weren't rounded mounds I'd have taken them for large, extra-wide floor planks.

In the furthest corner of a room that was framed with

dirt was the start of a trunk of a tree. The bark looked smooth and gray in the dim light and it was wider than anything I'd ever seen. It probably took the entire back part of the courtyard if it went up through the ground, yet I'd never seen it.

"This is the first tree," Zachary said. "It has other names, but it's the easiest to say and the one I use."

I looked at him, puzzled.

"To last this long, it has power. Some people are called to be caretakers but some of us live as its equals." Zachary was looking at the tree the way he'd looked at me in my bedroom this afternoon, only, dare I say, with more affection.

I backed up towards the door. I wished that Richard really had been in the room. While he was strange and rather harsh, I suddenly had a feeling he had my best interests at heart.

Zachary's words had put a chill through me. I knew nothing about any power but I had no desire to find out what Zachary thought it could do or what was required in order for him to utilize that power.

The door swung inwards, nearly hitting me. I jumped to the side. Richard came back in.

"Stand back," Zachary ordered. "I will utilize the powers of the tree."

"Have you slept with him?" Richard demanded of me, ignoring Zachary.

"What?"

"If there is some part of him inside you, if you have been sexually active, then he can use that as part of the physical sacrifice he must make."

I opened my mouth but nothing came out.

Richard's face turned grimmer than it already was before he turned to Zachary.

"You don't need this power. There are practical things we can do."

"Like borrow money from Naomi the Golden Girl?" Zachary snapped. "I put everything into this place and nothing has gone right."

Richard sighed. "I warned you that the number of people up there would upset things. Cam and I have been working to keep her calm. Even Naomi has been working with us. You yourself know how hard it's been to try and keep her on an even keel with the visitors...."

Zachary turned on Richard glaring at him. "You keep saying I can't use this power. But I can harness that power which will force her to calm down for decades."

"The sacrifice isn't worth it," Richard said.

"I say it is."

"I'm here to stop you." Richard pushed Zachary away from the tree, towards me.

"Run towards the hotel and out. The path to the woods is too dangerous. If you have to claw through the door, do it," Richard ordered, looking at me.

Zachary stumbled back towards him.

The earth shook.

I moved to the door, which opened when I pulled.

I ran into the corridor.

This just wasn't not wanting to be in the basement with a potentially crazy man, this was me not wanting to be some sort of sacrifice.

I imagined my womb being pulled from my body to take his cells with it because that was why we'd had sex. He'd planned this all along.

It's probably why Richard had chosen that evening to change rooms. He knew it would bother Zachary and keep him from trying to seduce me or allowing me to seduce him.

The door into the main rooms of the subbasement was still shut tight.

I pushed on it, trying to break it down but nothing seemed to work.

I pounded on it.

I wished I'd still had the flashlight, not so much for light but for the weight that might break through the boards.

I heard something echo on the other side of the door, as if someone was pounding their way in.

Finally my hand broke through the wood.

I felt the broken boards splinter and slash my hand.

Warm blood flowed down my my fingers but I was still able to get them around the splintered board and pull.

I pulled off a few more boards until I could slip out. Soft hands pulled at me.

I tried to rear back.

"It's me," Chris said, softly. "Hurry."

I let him help me through the door.

I noticed it wasn't latched in any manner I could understand. It just wouldn't open.

"We need to go," I said.

Chris, fortunately, had a flashlight, not as bright as the electric lantern Zachary had used but powerful enough that we could see where we were going. It was helpful even though the rooms were lit with a half light from the dim bulbs. I was glad of it.

He shone it ahead of me as I led the way through the room towards where I believed the stairs were.

The rooms seemed bigger now and it took me nearly as long to run through them as it had to walk through them Zachary.

It was like being in a nightmare.

There was only me, the circle of light from the flashlight, and Chris's breathing.

I kept on running.

Just as I got the doorway that would take me into the room with the generator, I saw Zachary up ahead waiting for me.

I stopped. "No." I looked again, hoping it was my imagination.

It couldn't be Zachary.

He was back behind me.

I'd felt as if every second had been an hour but that had to be my mind playing tricks right?

The skunk smell came back more strongly than ever and I started to gag. I heard Chris moving behind me.

I turned to see what he would do, but Chris wasn't there. Only Zachary who was in front of me and behind me.

I turned again and the person in front of me was gone.

I started to run towards the room with the generator.

Maybe I was hallucinating again.

A tree root broke through the floor and grabbed me.

The roots were brown hands, long and slender like Chris's hands.

My heart nearly stopped.

"What have you done?" I screamed back at Zachary.

"Oh, nothing permanent. The tree won't let me kill a caretaker but it doesn't care if I disable him. Come back there with me, Becca."

"Are you crazy?" I was pulling away from the root as hard as I could.

The roots were thick and clung tightly around my ankle, digging in hard.

If I managed to slip out I'd be injured and bleeding at best. At worst, it would have pulled off my foot.

"Not at all," Zachary said. "I'm merely using all the abilities at hand."

"I am not going to let you kill me," I screamed.

"You wouldn't die," Zachary said. "Yes, it would be painful and there's a chance you wouldn't have children, but the tree doesn't take full lives."

I shook my head. I wasn't going to trust him.

"The more you fight, the more of you it will take, though."

Now there was a threat to give me pause. At the same time, would he let me go if this happened? Would I ever get out of this place?

"And think about your friend, Chris. The tree won't want him, but accidents happen in sub-basements like this and I'm insured against intruders," Zachary said calmly.

I paused to glare at him, wondering what he had done with Chris.

Chapter 22

I pulled against the tree root one more time, trying to think.

"Dad?" I heard a voice calling. Cam.

Zachary looked towards the voice and frowned.

I heard scruffling along the floor, as if Cam were coming into the room. I hoped he could help me but worried Zachary might just knock him out.

"He's not here!" Zachary finally called.

He reached me and grabbed my arm.

The moment his hands grabbed my shoulders, the root let go of my ankle.

Zachary pulled me up. I fought him.

My fighting did little but distract me from what was happening around me.

I couldn't hear if Cam were coming.

"Zachary's hurt him! And a guest!" I shouted in case Cam could still hear me. "Get help!"

I had no idea if Cam could even hear me much less help me.

The room darkened as if the lights were dimming.

It got cold.

I pushed away from Zachary, who was holding me only lightly.

I realized we were in a primeval forest.

The large tropical plant leaves towered over my head. The basement might have been under the night sky instead of just a deep cellar.

There was no path.

I smelled skunk and something musky. At least I wouldn't gag.

Rustling came from ahead of us.

I turned but Zachary hadn't moved. He looked worried.

"What is it?" I demanded.

He didn't look at me.

He was looking towards the rustling sound. I turned that way, waiting.

The large frond that had been curved over my head started to move slightly, then with more agility.

The smell became stronger. A snout that was probably at the level of Zachary's head pushed the fronds apart.

The creature moved further in. It was pale beige, lightly scaled. It put me in mind of an anteater. Beady black eyes stared at Zachary.

He grabbed me and pushed me in front of him, like a shield, as we backed away from the creature.

After a few feet, hidden behind fronds that grew taller than I could see, Zachary turned around, pushing me forward. I was struck by whip-like leaves that left my face covered in sap.

Zachary came to a halt before too long. He pulled me back, forcing me to turn to face him.

"You had to go calling to him," he snarled. "Do you know what he can do?"

"Who? Cam?" I had no idea why he was so angry.

"I owe the tree something to get power. The more power I need, the more I owe. I needed you for what I wanted. Now I'll need you to pay it back for any power I use here. Don't you get it?"

"No." I mean, let's be real. I didn't live in a world where magical tree creatures offered magic in exchange for body parts.

That just wasn't normal. No more than it wasn't normal to go running around in a primeval forest.

The light around me dimmed more, like the sun was setting in the primeval forest and we were back in the sub-basement, not far from where the armoire sat blocking the door I had broken through.

I tried to pull away from Zachary but his arm was once more like a vise.

He practically dragged me forward.

I grabbed the armoire.

I was not going back in that hallway.

I screamed for all I was worth.

Not that I thought it would do any good. If Cam had heard me and was inclined to help, he would have heard me earlier.

There was no way a scream would reach the guests upstairs.

I imagined my voice being sucked up into the tree like water going into the roots.

The leaves that I hadn't seen would unfurl and they would be the wide fronds of the tropical plants I had just seen.

I heard something behind us and I tried to turn my head.

Zachary was prying my fingers from the armoire and

pulling me away. I thought I saw someone hurrying towards us but I lost my grip on the armoire.

I started looking for something else to grab to slow us even further.

The door was coming closer.

I still had time to stop, but there was nothing in the hallway that I could use.

I remembered the roots coming up to stop me.

If Cam hurried, maybe he had a weapon.

"Zachary!" It wasn't Cam's voice I heard.

It was a woman's.

"I'm the heir!" Zachary called back. "You can't touch me."

Naomi walked around the corner, avoiding the armoire, which was heavy enough that I hadn't even jostled it with my grabbing.

She shook her head at Zachary. "Let her go."

"She's mine. I can use her."

"The guardians have determined she's not to be used," Naomi said quietly. "You saw it."

"They haven't told me that. Not in so many words. So long as Richard doesn't speak the words in front of the tree, I can't be held accountable. And I made sure he won't be speaking them any time soon."

Naomi blanched, pausing. There was a look of horror on her face. "You didn't kill him?" Barely above a whisper.

Zachary snorted and shook his head. "Death isn't the only way to keep someone speaking. I knocked him out. He's tied up and I've made certain he can't talk for a long while."

"It won't work. The tree has always had the final say and knowing what would be said if you hadn't kept the guardian from speaking is a line it's not likely to let you cross," Naomi said calmly.

"Once I get this power, that won't matter," Zachary told her. "Not so much. Even if she has to take a finger or something further of mine, I'll let her. Then you can have the tree. I just want my hotel and I want it to be a financial success."

"Don't do it." Naomi stood facing him, her arms crossed.

Zachary pulled me back towards him, pushing me into the hallway.

The door behind which the tree huddled looked closer to the entry to the corridor than it had earlier.

It stood open, the blackness beckoning like a maw.

I tried to grab the broken boards that had freed me earlier but I only got a handful of splinters.

Naomi walked quickly forward, but then she stopped, as if she'd come to a wall.

She pressed her hands against the air like she was being met with a door.

I screamed again but knew she couldn't hear me. She was trapped and would not come to my rescue.

Like Cam, in all likelihood.

Like Chris, or so I hoped.

Zachary dragged me down the hallway.

I tried digging my fingers into the dirt walls, scraping my fingernails off, tearing the skin at the tips.

Zachary didn't even slow.

All too soon we were back at the door.

Zachary loosened his hold on me a little when he closed the door behind us.

I pulled away to run but tripped on a tree root that had come up through the dirt.

"Don't even try it," Zachary said. "You've cost me enough tonight. More than you can ever know."

I looked around in the room, hoping I could get close to Richard, but I didn't see him.

Zachary stopped, staring into a corner.

I looked but saw nothing.

I pulled away and his hand just dropped.

I backed out of the room.

Nothing stopped me.

I pulled open the door, which opened in my hands so quickly I almost hit myself.

Naomi stood at the other side, hand out, clearly pushing the door inward.

"Are you okay?" she asked quietly.

"For now," I said. "I still want out of here. Out of the hotel. And there's another guest named Chris who was with me, but he's gone now."

"Cam's with him," Naomi said. "Come on."

I glanced back and I saw Richard in the corner.

There was something shadowy near him. It looked like a shadow of the tree in the other corner but it was reaching out to Zachary, oddly.

Naomi sighed. "Hurry. This is not something you'll want to be around for, particularly since this afternoon."

I didn't have to be told twice.

Naomi set a fast pace. Nothing grabbed at my ankles and the floor stayed flat dirt. No doors blocked our way.

When we came to the room with the ancient furnace, I saw Cam kneeling on the floor. Chris was there, trying to sit up.

"There you go," Cam said. "Can you stand?"

Chris saw me. "You're okay?"

"She's okay for now," Naomi said. "But she needs to get away from here as quickly as possible."

Chris stood, and though he shook his head as if he

were dizzy, he made for the far door, the one that held the generator.

Cam held him up at first, but soon enough he appeared stronger on his feet.

I followed with Naomi pushing my back.

After opening the door to the stairs, Cam hung back, letting us all go through. Then I heard the door closed and he wasn't with us.

"Should he come, too?" I asked.

"Never mind," Naomi said. "He'll be fine."

"What's he doing?" I asked Naomi as she pushed me up the next flight of stairs so hard that I nearly stumbled into Chris.

"Not now," Naomi said. "I can feel the energy building and I want you off this property before they do anything."

Chris opened the door to the first floor. Naomi pushed us both along the corridor so quickly I was practically running.

"Do you have your car keys?" Naomi asked Chris.

"I do," he said.

"We need to get her out of here, as far as you can. You can come back for her things," Naomi said, looking at Chris.

The older gentleman that I'd noticed around the hotel was sitting in the lobby near the tall fireplace. He looked surprised to see us. I wondered what we looked like.

I had nothing with me, not even my purse.

Chris pushed open the main doors and then we were in the parking lot.

He led me over to an old Jeep that had clearly seen plenty of wear and tear. It was dark enough that I couldn't quite tell the color, only that it was a dark-colored Jeep.

Chris helped me in. He would have helped Naomi but she was already in the back seat.

He ran around the front to reach his side.

He started the car and the back wheels screeched as we tore out of the parking space. He raced along the gravel parking lot, not even slowing when he saw another car heading towards us.

The startled guests must have slammed on their brakes and sat staring at us long after we'd passed them.

Clearly he'd taken Naomi's words to heart.

We were up the hill and around the bend in very short order.

Chris was flying down the road so quickly I worried we'd never make it. It made Zachary's wild drive along the private entrance look like slow meander under the trees.

Chris didn't even look around when he screamed out of the gates and took the main road towards town. He passed a couple of cars, going off onto the wide shoulder to overtake them because there was traffic going outbound as well. When we got to the main highway out of town, he slowed some and seemed to breathe again.

"What happened to you?" I asked Chris.

"Something hit me on the back of the head. I woke up and found that young man trying to wake me."

"Cam's a good man," Naomi said quietly.

"I liked him," I replied, thinking about it. He had seemed like such a normal teenager. "What happened?" I turned in my seat to look at Naomi.

"Cam slowed Zachary down by sending him through the portal. Because of that, it seems Richard was able to explain to the tree what was going on. The tree, or the god that inhabits that tree, clearly didn't like the story. They are preparing to cut Zachary off from his inheritance."

"What will that do to him?" I asked.

Naomi sighed. I was waiting to hear her answer when I got

the worse cramp of my life. I'd had menstrual cramps since I was a teenager. This was nothing like that. This was a bend over, someone-is-slicing-me-open-with-a-knife-and-pulling-my-insides-out kind of a cramp. My body wasn't letting go easily. There was agony up and down my pelvic area.

The pain made me gasp. I would have screamed or cried but it took my breath away. Everything was focused on that lower part of my abdomen. I wondered if women felt like this giving birth. Tears were running down my face.

As quickly as it hit, it was gone. I gasped again, this time drinking in as much air as I could, as if I'd just run a marathon.

"Is it over?" Naomi asked.

"What?"

"Your pain?"

I nodded. Couldn't she tell?

"Good. I have heard that it can be far far worse than that. Richard has the histories and he's taught them to us, but I think there are some things you must experience for yourself, and I haven't."

"Well, it was bad enough here. If distance makes a difference, I wouldn't have wanted to be any closer."

"People have died because of it," Naomi said. "But the tree doesn't wait."

"What is it?" I asked. "What is that thing that you have there?"

Naomi didn't answer at first.

Chris glanced at her in the rearview mirror, then looked at me. His face was drawn with worry.

"How far do I keep going?" he asked.

"Perhaps find a hotel south of the town if you can," Naomi said. "I'll call Richard to come and get me. He'll also book us rooms so we don't need to worry about Becca not having an ID."

Naomi didn't say anything more.

"But what was that?" I asked again.

Chris glanced at me.

"That's the question, isn't it?" Naomi said, staring straight ahead. "I don't know. We don't understand it. It's just 'the tree.'" She made little finger quotes around the words.

"Somehow, my family is bonded to it. Each generation, defined when the person of the older generation has died, someone becomes a sort of companion to it. I can influence some things around the castle but only Zachary could influence everything."

"What do you mean, influence things?" I asked. "I've been thinking I'm going crazy there, seeing shadows and that dead pond...."

Naomi raised an eyebrow, no longer staring at nothing but looking at me. "Zachary had probably primed the tree, asking if mixing with you and your cells would be acceptable as a sacrifice, or more accurately, a 'meal' for when he needed power. The tree was checking you out. I'm surprised you saw the pond. I didn't think anyone besides the families could do that."

"I was there alone the first day and I saw it, but then it happened again with Zachary when we went walking."

Naomi shook her head. "No wonder he was willing to use you, despite everything. The tree would have given him just about anything after that. You might find that your family mixed with ours sometime in the last few centuries and you got the genetics that would have put you in line to be a companion."

"And Richard and Cam?"

"They're caretakers, although it might be more accurate to say guardians. They make sure the companion doesn't hurt the tree. And *hurt* is defined broadly. Letting anyone know about what the tree can do is considered hurting it."

"Aren't you hurting it by telling me?"

"I'm not yet the companion," Naomi said. "I can be talked to, but I doubt, given what you saw and what happened, that there will be anything but a warning."

"And you'll become the next companion after Zachary?"

"He's been severed from the tree now. Tomorrow Richard will go through the process of making me companion as I'm next in line. If I don't survive, then they'll find a next of kin."

"Companions don't always survive?" My voice squeaked.

I looked out the window to see the cars passing normally along the road. Maybe I'd wake up soon and find myself next to Zachary in bed and all of this would have been a dream.

Naomi shook her head. "Several of us have died. It's why the family has stayed small."

I was silent, thinking about what she'd said. I was still in shock. It wasn't real—except the blood on my fingers was. And I still remembered that pain.

"What about my car?" I asked. I didn't want to go back to the castle but I needed to know what garage my car was in. "When will it be ready?"

"It was ready this morning. Zachary just didn't want you going anywhere," Naomi said. "It was my first real indication of what he might be up to."

I watched fast food places pass by in the night, thankfully lighting everything up in a variety of colors, all modern and, while not beautiful by any means, normal.

It started to rain again, thick, heavy drops.

Naomi sighed. "I hate it when it rains around here. The tree both loves it and hates it. Things are going be very active at the castle. That's the main reason Zachary could never get the place off the ground. The tree gets so excited when there are lots of people around and it's a bit mischievous. Zachary would have been better to have tried to market the place as being haunted. He probably still can, I suppose."

"He'll still have the hotel?" Chris asked. "I mean, after what he did? He could have killed Becca, couldn't he?"

Naomi looked down at her hands. "The best we can do is un-bond him from the tree. Because he won't be a companion, nor will he be in line to be a companion, he won't remember the tree at all. He won't remember any of this. He'll know I inherited a spooky castle and let him try and make it a hotel. Richard's family is good about making sure that the door is hidden from anyone who shouldn't find it."

Chris snorted. "Seems like he got off easily for practically trying to kill someone."

"Most people don't die from the process Zachary was trying, although given that Becca was rather tuned in to the tree, she would have been harmed more than most. I expect the worst thing would have been that she was unable to have children, assuming it didn't drive her mad," Naomi said.

As if that was any comfort.

"Seems bad enough to me," Chris said.

The windshield wipers soothed me with their rhythmic hush. In no time we were just outside Asheville. Chris exited onto a main street and made a couple of turns. We ended up in front of a rather ordinary-looking rectangular hotel. It was one of the high-end chains that I normally wished I felt good about affording but didn't allow myself the luxury of.

"You'll be refunded in full for your stay," Naomi said. "It's the least I can do. Zachary won't remember you, exactly. If he sees you or if you come back to Kernroote, he'll know you, but he won't recognize your name. I'm not sure how he'll react if he sees you. It's possible it will bring it all back."

"No offense, but I'm completely fine letting you pick up my stuff and bring it here. I'm not that excited about going back."

Naomi nodded and smiled. "I'll get you checked in, seeing you have no ID or money. The first week here will be on me. Again, it's the least we can do."

"Thank you," I said. I wasn't ready to get home again. And I wasn't sure how I'd tell Kara about all of this.

Naomi had Chris wait while she went inside and started getting us checked in. She walked in holding her phone. I wondered if she was talking to Richard. Of course, how could she be talking to him already? Was he that fast?

It took her some time to come back out.

"Will you be okay?" Chris asked.

"I think so, now," I said. "I'll miss my phone and stuff, but at least I'm not at Kernroote right now."

"I could go back for it for you," Chris said. "So you'll have it tonight."

"I can wait for Cam and Naomi."

Chris breathed a sigh that sounded a lot like relief.

"I have to admit I wasn't all that thrilled about going back there. I might hunt up ghosts, but whatever you wandered into was not what I expected. I'm glad I could help out. And if you want to talk about your experience, I might not have been there but I saw enough to know whatever you described, you weren't crazy."

"Thank you," I said. "And thanks for offering even if you didn't want to go. That was nice."

Naomi came back out. She gestured to us and we both exited the Jeep.

"You have rooms up on the top floor. Booked for five days each under my name, Naomi Kerne. You shouldn't have any problems. Order room service or whatever you want, the card on file is good for it. I talked to Richard and he's sending Cam over to get me and he'll have both your things."

"He didn't have to do that," Chris said. "Not for me."

Naomi smiled. "Did you really want to go back?"

Chris shook his head.

"I didn't think so."

Naomi settled into a chair in the lobby to wait as Chris and I got into the elevator to take us to our rooms. I loved that it creaked and groaned a little as it went up, but the ride was smooth. I smelled citrus and chemical smells of cleanser along the hallways. In two places I heard the television playing much too loudly, and near my own room I heard someone start the water running.

"I love the noises," I said. "It was always too quiet at Kernroote."

Chris smiled. "You'll be okay alone? Do you need me to come in and watch while you sleep or anything?"

I shook my head. "Just let me know what your room number is in case anything weird happens and I have to call for help!"

It turned out he was across the hall. So no awkward adjoining rooms. Perhaps Naomi had thought of that or perhaps there was someone in the room next to mine. I went in to my room, looking around, pleased that everything about it, from the boring floral pictures to the plain white duvet, was so normal.

I had no pajamas, so I didn't know what to do with myself. I flopped back on the bed, trying to make sense of things. I must have dozed off because the next thing I knew there was a knock on my door.

I looked the peephole. Cam and Naomi were there with my luggage.

"I'm sorry we had to do that, Ms. Winter," Cam said, bringing in my luggage.

"Thank you for taking care of things when it counted," I said. "I suspect that what happened wasn't exactly your fault."

Cam shrugged.

Naomi was already knocking on Chris's door to offload his things from the cart they'd brought up. Both acted as though they were used to acting as bellboys. I hoped they wouldn't have to do that for Zachary as he ran the hotel.

Chris's hair was mussed when he came to the door so he must also have fallen asleep. His shirt was misbuttoned, but he gave me a smile when he saw me at the door while Cam brought in my bags.

Naomi handed me a map to the tire place. I could even walk there, although I had a feeling Chris would be more than happy to drive me.

Cam gave me a card for his father, in case there were any problems with my refund or if I needed anything further from them.

He handed one to Chris as well. "Sorry your stay didn't work out. I think Dad was hoping you'd find an ordinary ghost." Cam laughed while he wheeled the cart down the hall behind Naomi.

I raised an eyebrow.

"It's kind of a long story," Chris said. "Do you mind if I tell you over breakfast?"

I smiled, knowing I didn't mind at all. We set a time and I went back into my room.

I opened my laptop to make sure I still had my book. It was there. No strange messages waiting for me. And the words I had written didn't seem quite as inane as they had a few days ago. I sighed, closing it. Maybe I could finish it here, or at least get most of it done.

I looked out at the dark night, at the lights around Asheville twinkling, and listened to the people next door yell about the fact that he left the toilet seat up. I smiled. This was normal. I could write.

Maybe I'd even be able to incorporate Chris's story about hunting ghosts into the romance. After all, how many women fall for a ghost hunter?

About Bonnie Elizabeth

Bonnie Elizabeth could never decide what to do, so she wrote stories about amazing things and sometimes she even finished them.

While rejection stung her so badly in person, she spent most of her young life talking to cats and dogs rather than people, she was unusually resilient when it came to rejections on her writing, racking up a good number of them.

Floating through a variety of jobs, including veterinary receptionist, cemetery administrator, and finally acupuncturist, she continued to write stories.

When the internet came along (yes she's old), she started blogging as her cat, because we all know cats don't notice rejection. Then she started publishing.

Bonnie writes in a variety of genres. Her popular Whisper series is contemporary fantasy and her Teenage Fairy Godmother series is written for teens. She has published in a number of anthologies and is working on expanding her writing repertoire.

She lives with her husband (who talks less than she does) and her three cats, who always talk back.

Stay in Touch

Also by Bonnie Elizabeth

The Frost Witch Saga

October Snow
November Frost
December Storm

Appalachian Souls

Souls Lost
Souls Broken

The Ash Jericho Series

An Inheritance to Die For
A Discovery to Die For
A Distraction to Die For

The Whisper Novels

Whisper Bound
Taken by the Sound
An Air of Suspicion
Little Dog Lost
Death Interrupted

Down in Whisper

A Haunting Whisper

A Haunting Attraction

Secrets Not Whispers

Only Human

Other Novels

One Bad Wish

Sun Spot Magic

Ghosts from the Past

Unnatural Secrets

Shadows of Solstice

Find them all at your favorite bookseller or check us out at
MyBigFatOrangeCat.com